T0329408

On A Sad Weather-Beaten Couch

Sanya Osha

Langaa Research & Publishing CIG
Mankon, Bamenda

Publisher:
Langaa RPCIG
Langaa Research & Publishing Common Initiative Group
P.O. Box 902 Mankon
Bamenda
North West Region
Cameroon
Langaagrp@gmail.com
www.langaa-rpcig.net

Distributed in and outside N. America by African Books Collective
orders@africanbookscollective.com
www.africanbookscollective.com

ISBN: 9956-762-42-3

DISCLAIMER
All views expressed in this publication are those of the author and do
not necessarily reflect the views of Langaa RPCIG.

Ade Bantan lay on the sofa in his girlfriend's living room fanning himself and trying to seize upon a measure of coolness. He had nowhere to go. He had nothing to do. He just had to remain on the couch until Enitan, his girlfriend returned from work. Day in and day out, that was what his routine had become. He would lie on the couch or on the floor without a shirt, fervently hoping that a baleful cloud did not descend upon him and that the feeling of not wanting to endure yet another day did not incapacitate him.

When such a cloud did descend, Ade Bantan had had not even the will to weep. If he were to hold up his arm, it would drop limply, as if it were not part of his body at all. When that happened, he knew that he was in trouble. Real trouble.

He had no money to waste on shrinks. Even if he had, what good would that do? Most shrinks had no time to spend nursing a patient back to health. They were too busy trying to sustain their careers, too engrossed with the challenge of keeping the funds rolling in. They were too busy to listen in order to find out what was really happening. Too busy to think. Too busy for everything. And so, Ade Bantan could not afford to go through the ordeal of passing through the hands of a bunch of lousy shrinks.

If word got around that he had problems with mind or in his head, he would have a lot of explaining to do. He just couldn't be bothered with the rigmarole. He couldn't be bothered with all that crap. So he would lie on the couch in semi-darkness as the slow poisonous tide of woe welled up within him. So no one could see the extent of his pain. So no one could sense that he was gradually poisoning himself. No one knew he was having daily conversations with his departed relatives and with his own death.

No one knew the devastating power of his unseen guests. No one knew a damn thing about him.

And so, he had become his own shrink, holding internal monologues about missed opportunities, paths not taken, friendships broken, thresholds not crossed, crack-ups of the heart and balls, and a whole litany of other failures. How many doors had closed before him that he did bother to shove for fear of yet another failure? How many opportunities had he merely walked away from? It was impossible to tell. Too many in fact. But in the arrogance of youth, you believe that there will be more opportunities, more doors beckoning. You could always say fuck that route and take the next one. It was as simple as that. So you fetch you next mug of coffee and life continues as it always does if you have the patience to look around the corner of thorns and darkness.

At thirty-seven, Ade Bantan no longer saw doors beckoning to him. He could only see corners of darkness and thorns and dead elongated, rotting bodies that had crashed in motor car accidents along the way. It tore at his entrails for such images to drift through his mind with such mind-searing vividness. Awful. Really bad. These are the sorts of images that made him appear to be lost when Enitan entertained guests, sitting with his arm propping his chin up like a dispirited philosopher relieving himself on heap of rubbish in a slum.

No one could understand him once he got into that sort of mood. He did not fully understand such baleful moods himself. They had been visiting him for months on end. He began to think that he would have to endure them for the rest of his wretched existence. An existence marked with ominous silences, gaps, and deceptions. It wasn't a good idea to attempt to connect some of those troublesome dots in his small journey of life. If he did, Enitan would reject him, her sisters would jeer, her brother would scoff at him, and her numerous relatives might threaten to beat him up.

Everyone believed Ade Bantan was a great painter destined for impressive things. He had met Enitan, barely out of her teens, fifteen years before, when she came to an art exhibition in which some of his work was displayed. Then, he had managed to impress a posse of art patrons who jostled for his attention. He would never forget the red plaid micro miniskirt she wore, her fashionable white shirt, and black flat shoes. She wore a few colorful bangles she'd bought from some Fulani traders. Nothing expensive, but she was cool. She had a terrific figure then, which she managed to maintain all these years later. For some reason, on that first day, she kept hovering around him trying to catch his attention. By then, Ade Bantan had had several glasses of fine red wine. His head was buzzing with the goodness of life. Yes, life was wonderful. Let's eat, drink, and fuck until the end of time. Such was his mood that night.

Eventually, toward the end of the evening's proceedings, Ade Bantan and Enitan got to talking. She asked him questions. What does it take to become an artist? Do you make a lot of money selling art? How does one go about being an artist? Did you think I had it in me to become an artist? Several times, Ade Bantan had no clue how to reply.

Ade Bantan looked artsy then; dreadlocks, florid shirts made in Banjul and Dakar, Italian sandals, French cologne, earrings, and metrosexual make-up. It was his time to act, to be cool. Enitan was probably more interested in his get-up than his art. She liked the way he looked and thought he would be an interesting fuck. By the time they left the art gallery, she was already deep kissing him. Raymond Ragshad, a friend and fellow artist, whispered in Ade Bantan's ear:

3

This girl would fight to marry you and then get a baby with another man and present it to you as yours. Mark my words.

Raymond Ragshad's foresight and clairvoyance were simply remarkable. At that age, Enitan had more stuff in her panties than ants. It didn't matter to Ade Bantan then. Why should it? He was out to have fun and good fun had nothing to do with morals. He made a date to see Enitan the next day before they boarded separate public buses to go home.

They met at lunchtime at a cramped eatery a few blocks from the art gallery. There were only a couple of people around, so much the better to concentrate on each other. She asked him the same questions she had asked the previous night. What does it take to be an artist? Do you make a lot of money selling art? How does one go about being an artist? Did he think she had it in her to become one?

Only this time, she could focus on his eyes, arrest them from drifting. Not that there was much to distract his attention. It appeared the eatery was having its last gasps before dying an unmourned death. The tables were unbalanced, the garish red paint on the walls advertised the Coca Cola trademark over and over again. Only one waitress catered to everybody, and the meals were lousy. The specialty was cold rice served with bits and ends of beef dipped in stew. The stew was invariably cold. There were many high-rises under construction nearby, making the din quite loud. The traffic too was heavy with bus conductors yelling their lungs out and drivers hooting for no reason at all. Haywire capitalism at its worst. Kill and eat your brethren or be killed and eaten by them. What kept the eatery alive for so long was that it was dead cheap. Also, it was a convenient spot for married people to have assignations with their lovers away from prying eyes. That was the lousy eatery's biggest selling point.

On that day, Ade Bantan did not know that it was already that bad. He didn't realize that the cars that hooted incessantly were grinding the bones and clotted blood of dead souls underneath. He wasn't yet aware that the high-rises that scrambled to drag down the skies were fed with the bodies of half-dead men by the hundreds everyday. He didn't know that each and every building along the streets was a funeral house, that the funeral houses emitted mutilated souls at dawn and ate raw human flesh for dinner. He was blind to the fact that no one was exempt from the plunder, murder, and hypocritical complicity; no one was free from the cycle of eating shit for breakfast, lunch, and dinner and then sitting on the throne of shit at night. Everyone was running on the treadmill of shit production either as a consumer or as a producer.

If Ade Bantan had aready learned this vital lesson by the time when he first met Enitan, then perhaps his spirit would not not be so heavy now; perhaps he would not always appear to be a defeated thinker on a pile of shit in a slum while others laughed and made jokes; perhaps he would be able to bear the seemingly interminable journey of a smile from the depths of his belly to the glassy façade of his teeth.

But at that moment in their lives, Ade Bantan still had the dubious privilege of dining with the bloated shit producers who were his patrons and Enitan ate shit for breakfast, lunch, and dinner. She just wanted to get out of that blind cycle of abuse so that she could see clearly for once. She had a great hunger for sight and she was ready to cling to anyone who could guide her to the precipice of sight. Her spirit sensed that it was trapped in the gorge of blindness. Deep in the gorge of wailing, flailing spirits, souls groaned and moaned,

5

slithered in mud and sludge, expired in tunnels without ends, fought for gasps of air that burned like fire, and became extinct like heavy tadpoles on the slimy muck of night.

We drown in our own tears. Consolation abandons us, leaving us alone to console other souls plagued with the misfortunes of life.

This was the condition Enitan was struggling to escape. This was the condition that fed her hunger for sight as she groped about blindly for a foothold, an anchor to secure her from the unfathomable expanse of sludge in airless space. Who could blame her? It was hot, dark, and destructive in that space where one could expire in the nameless distance between life and death on a waiting list where the damned invariably went missing in transit.

On that day, Ade Bantan had not yet known the devastation caused by muck and airless spaces. After all, those who produced shit invited him to their tables and drawing rooms. He played with their children and joked with their wives. He was fine—for now. He didn't quite understand the ravages of desperation—yet. Desperation was something he came across in books, newspapers, and casual conversations that he would soon forget. Desperation was for those who groveled in slums and became deaf with grime in their ears. No it was not for him and needn't be. He was okay and cool for now.

As Ade Bantan and Enitan slowly sipped their soft drinks amid the noise of construction workers and traffic, a bond started to form between them. Her sultry looks had finally caught his eye. She hoped he would be more than the boy he resembled; she hoped he would be a real man who could take care of her; lead her to that precipice of sight and light that she sought; remove the thick grime from her ears; give her the family she had never really had; build something with her from the air of life; grow old with her amid the laughter and activities of their children and grandchildren; and finally, she would bow before the airplane of life in a time of dusk and kiss the tired soil beneath. Then she could claim the ultimate victory over the adversities that had dogged her throughout her life and robbed her of innocence from her cradle.

If only her life could turn out as she had envisioned. If only she could experience the grace and pleasures of a smile at dusk. Something within her worried her that those dreams were too far-fetched, that the damage had already been done, that the pathways that led to her grave were littered with frank, businesslike smirks, bitten lips, ambushed bodies and plans, innumerable betrayals, backs bearing plunged knives, hypocrites, day-old flesh, layers of deception over deception, masquerades that traumatize children, and death that demands endless repetitions. But Enitan was a determined personality; she would fight because she had no choice, because there was nothing else she could do. She had to fight because she had seen hope flash a set of gleaming white teeth.

As she sat on the edge of the wobbly bench, Enitan continued to look into Ade Bantan's eyes for vestiges of hope, for something to cling to. Ade Bantan was talking casually, trying to make her laugh. He hoped she was besotted with him. Finally, he said to her,

You know what you need? A good fuck. That would solve all your problems.

You think so?

Yeah. I'm sure. I'm never wrong on such matters.

7

The sun was setting by the time they were ready to leave the eatery that was on the brink of death. Rush hour traffic had piled up. Automobile fumes clogged the air; shops were closing for the day; masses of grumpy, tired people were returning to their various holes for the night. As they walked to the bus stop, Ade Bantan held Enitan's hand. She didn't resist; in fact, she appeared to be comfortable.

Ade Bantan gradually got a hard-on, almost breaking out of his pants, unbearable. He urgently needed relief. Simple as that. No complications, no sentimental tears of joy, no hugs and kisses to nurture or cement any emotional bond. Just good old plain fucking to assuage a cock gone astray. With almost every throb, he squeezed Enitan's hand harder. When they got to the bus stop, he asked if she wanted to come to his place for a drink.

I don't know.

Make up your mind. It's not that difficult.

Ok, I could come by, but only for a few minutes because I have to get home on time.

Sure girl. No problem.

They boarded a death trap of a bus, bodies packed like sardines amid the reek of sweat and squalor. There was no avoiding the gloom of the suffocating smell. Two live goats bleated at the back of the bus. The conductor was yelling for no reason. The driver was smoking a cigarette and blowing the smoke out of the window, but a gale kept blowing the smoke back inside. Three fat women sat behind Ade Bantan and Enitan. Their faces looked even more squashed from the lack of space.

One of the passengers carried a boy about two years old, who was wailing with snot running out of his nose into his mouth. His mother sucked some of the snot out of his nose and spat it through the window, nearly smearing a street peddler, who was selling wrist watches and sunglasses. He barely jumped out of the way of the jet of snot. In anger, he swore at the fat woman.

The bus made its slow crawl through peddlers selling biscuits, fizzy drinks, plantain and potato crisps, melting ice cream, and other things to keep the jaws busy. Along the way, broken-down cars caused more traffic commotion. In the midst of the noise, automobile fumes, swearing voices, and a million other crazy things, Ade Bantan held onto Enitan's hand. His hard-on hadn't quite subsided.

Ade Bantan sat behind the conductor, next to the door. The conductor sat on a heated ledge just behind the pair of front seats. He stank terribly and his clothing, mere scraps, was filthy. He wore a dark blue waist-coat that appeared to have been picked from a garbage dump. It was hard to tell the color of his shorts because of its confusing history of grime. Due to lack of space, one of the conductor's knees was brushing against Ade Bantan's groin. The conductor's musty odor almost choked him. Ade Bantan couldn't wait to get home and have a bath. Every time he squeezed Enitan's hand, he felt some slight relief. Eventually, they disembarked at a bus stop about half a mile from where he lived.

There was also a traffic jam in the neighborhood. Ade Bantan lived in an area that used to be middle class. But corrupt city planners had thrown order and decency to the dogs. Illegal shacks and settlements were threatening to take over the area. Electricity had become scarce due to numerous illegal connections. Refuse mounted underneath bridges and on the streets. Mentally ill and homeless people jostled with automobiles for space on the streets. Gangsters smoked marijuana in bars. Buildings and the streets were falling into acute decay. People sometimes fainted in the streets from the stench of refuse. Day became night and night became day.

After spending more than hour avoiding pushcart drivers and masses of aggrieved pedestrians, AdeBantan and Enitan reached a spot three hundred meters from where he lived. By then, the final rays of the sun had disappeared. Enitan drew back and said she couldn't go on any longer. That puzzled Ade Bantan. His hard-on had started to hurt and the frenzy of his imagination was causing him irregular heartbeats. No song could provide him with the sort of relief he needed. No birth of the cool could chill him out.

What's wrong baby? Why are you changing your mind?

It's late and I have to get back home or else my uncle will be angry with me.

You're only going to spend a few minutes; please let's go.

No. I can't. My uncle would be annoyed.

Ade Bantan held her hand tighter and tried to pull her along. She resisted vehemently and drew away. He could see there was no point in trying to convince her. She had made up her mind. She didn't want to sleep over at the first available opportunity. She didn't want him to think she was cheap. But she also saw through the superficiality and artificiality of such moral hogwash. It was all a load of bullshit. She would fuck whomever she wanted at any fucking

10

time she wished, and it's nobody's business what she does. That was her code, the code that provided her with her truth, her foundation that provided her with her shit. But knowing that the world was full of bullshit, in order to make some progress, she sometimes had to peddle shit for shit. She had sensed a glimmer of hope in Ade Bantan's carefree eyes. She would hang around long enough to see if he could take her to a peak from where she could see beyond the shit.

When Enitan finally slept with Ade Bantan, he reached new levels of sensual pleasure. She had a gift that sent him into rapture, a body whose language spoke directly to him, and in whose depths he could lose himself. Sexually, he had found his perfect match. She stayed for days amid the jumble of unfinished paintings, brushes, and open tubes of paint. He forgot about work. He was preoccupied with studying the contours of her bum under a couple of light blue sheets as she slept. He imagined her lovely breasts that were concealed from him as she lay face-down. She slept with her legs wide apart and her hair all over the place. He studied her various sleeping poses and constructed an assemblage of images to etch in his memory. Those images were music and he had to find lyrics for them. Once he did, the images would be forever implanted in his memory.

What was she dreaming about? Was she dreaming of canvases, brushes, and watercolors? Of the mysteries and rebellions of paint? Of images created out of the rage of madness? Was she fantasizing about finding a pathway to his soul just as their bodies had found a fortunate symmetry? Was she dreaming of making a home with him that would be blessed with joyous voices and calm, easy temperaments? Of taking a long cruise with him along the river of fuck down to the dusty country of dusk? He had ripples of gladness in his belly imagining that they shared similar dreams.

In those early days, Ade Bantan also lived with his uncle and his family, as she lived with hers. He had a room of his own so he could bring his lovers home. He had lost his father when he was two, and his father's elder brother had volunteered to bring him up after his mother remarried and settled in England. From time to time, she sent him money for paint, brushes, and canvases. But he felt alienated from everyone in his family now, from his uncle and aunt, and from his brood of cousins.

Painting had led him to the road he travelled now. He discovered a language only he reveled in, and which made living worthwhile in spite of the countless hassles. Painting provided him with both the power of individual illumination and the lucidity of madness.

As dogs barked, goats bleated, and horses neighed, he felt that he had discovered fields of deep silence via the instrumentality of paint. His sudden discovery nearly led to the total loss of his self. Amid the preoccupations of dogs, goats, and horses, he had found a solitary language that unfurled amid vast silences in the clouds. But for language to accomplish full form, for it to become fully defined and find a worthy place among the living, it had to be shared within at least a small community of outcasts.

The outcasts would be the footsoldiers at the gates of the fortress keeping away Neanderthals intent on ravaging the queen because they do not understand the mysterious language. It was the duty of the diligent footsoldiers to keep the barbarians at bay even they as scraped shit from their hairy arses to fling it at the golden gates.

In a bid to protect the queen and her mysterious language, Ade Bantan neglected the requirement to find a community of outcasts for the newfound dialect. The seed had germinated, but it required adequate nourishment for the seedling to flourish into a full-blown language. In the giddiness caused by the birth of the dialect, he had forgotten to plant the dialect, even on the seemingly barren tract of land belonging to a band of outcasts, so that it could grow.

In his euphoria, Ade Bantan thought that after being tossed around on a sea of tribulations, he had finally reached a firm shore populated by illustrious personages. This seemingly simple mistake would cost him dearly. The difference between success and failure was as enormous as the disparity between a seed and a plant. Between them lay an entire universe of transformation, in which stood the polarities between life and death, sea and land, mountains and skies. In not traversing the expanse of this immense divide, he had lost the secret of metamorphosis. In this regard, he hoped Enitan would turn out to be the handmaiden of the lost dialect, the tongue that patiently awaited the ethereal, transporting kiss of the ocean.

Both of them were in search of missing pieces to the puzzles of their lives. Both yearned for completeness in different ways. Only Ade Bantan didn't suffer from acute material deprivation. His art had brought him into circles that guaranteed him a modest meal ticket. He did not suffer from acute moral and spiritual blindness. Instead, he suffered from chronic light-headedness. It would be a joke if he died from unexplained vertigo.

Connecting with Enitan was his faint-hearted attempt to surmount the ridicule of being a victim of vertigo. Ade Bantan, someone once told him, you will die of joy and that would be a great tragedy. When the bouts of vertigo began, Ade Bantan's art started to fail. His inspiration dried up and the unused dialect remained locked away in a fortress filled with cobwebs, where lived a queen pining away in a state of mourning. That was when his troubles began; he wasn't making money anymore, and because he was no longer productive, his patrons began to doubt his talent. Should he just walk into land occupied by outcasts until he was swallowed up by the night? Should he engineer his disappearance from the face of the earth? Or should he join the world of hypocrites living on compost until he burst at the seams? And then, when he expired as a result of the unbearable dead-weight of bullshit piled upon him, the mourners could consume his prostrate corpse. Corpses feeding on corpses. Corpses engaging in rituals of sex. Corpses united to violate the inglorious pomposity of life. Corpses in dark long robes in a death factory in a silent ceremony of congratulations. Corpses laboring in factories of boredom tending to every routine with the strictness and precision of executioners. Corpses everywhere. Zombies. Corpses as fathers of the nation. Corpses disguised in robes of laugher and gaiety. Corpses in the interminable ritual of death and unbearable loss.

Ade Bantan was certain that Enitan wouldn't follow his dark line of thought even though she came from the same place of dark sludge. She had no choice in where her cradle had been placed, but she had a say in choosing the corner of the earth she would make her own. She hungered for sight and light, and if anyone impeded her in her quest, she would reject them outright.

He spent the entire day walking about waiting for nightfall. When he returned to his room, he found Enitan awake in front of the dressing mirror regarding herself. She wore only a pair of white panties and a black bra. Some of her hair was falling over her face. To Ade Bantan, she looked gorgeous. He grabbed her from behind and smothered her neck and shoulders with kisses. She hunched her shoulders in pleasure and then suddenly looked earnest once more.

I look old, very old.

What do you mean?

Can't you see for yourself? I look old and perhaps ugly.

No my dear, you look fabulous. I could fuck you until the end of eternity.

Without another word, Enitan slipped off her panties and unhooked her bra. A body blessed by goddesses stood stark naked before him. How was he supposed to manage such a sumptuous feast from the deities? He'd already had his fill of her. She had given him everything and more. He would have been quite content with engaging in nonsensical prattle as days passed, grasses turned brown in fields, and trees shed their leaves. He would have been cool with all the slow unhindered changes of nature.

In spite of his state of utter physical exhaustion, he dared not refuse the feast; he dared not annoy the goddesses. If they had invited him to fuck, fuck he would. If it were his destiny to expire on a throne of thighs and breasts, then so be it.

Enitan lay sprawled on the bed. They made love. Many minutes passed. Then, she rose and said she was going home.

Aren't you going to wait till after dinner?

No, I'm not hungry. Besides, I've got to see my uncle; he will be waiting for me.

When can I visit your place?

You're free to visit anytime.

One day, Ade Bantan went into town looking for Enitan's place. She lived in a congested locale with open sewers close to the streets. Virtually every house was running a business of some sort; rice, palm oil, vegetable oil, beans, cassava flakes, bean cakes, beer, candy, cigarettes, marijuana, illegal medicines, herbs, ointments, lotions for snake bite, love portions, laxatives of all sorts, concoctions for back ache, candles, and insecticides. There were hairdressers hard at work on porches, shoe shine boys busy at every other house, liquor stores, bars, and restaurants. Noise and commotion filled the streets. By the time he finally found the house where Enitan lived, he was giddy with the assault of sounds, sights, and smells. He was overwhelmed by the riotous mix of life and swirling colors. Apart from the buzz in his ears he was covered with a thin coat of black dust. He asked a boy playing in front of the building if Enitan lived there.

Yes.

Please can you get her?

The boy dashed into the building screaming Enitan's name. Ade Bantan stood waiting by the old gate of the building. He needed to sit down, have a cool drink, and catch his breath.

Enitan emerged from the building carrying a toddler by her side. She was wearing a skimpy pair of shorts beneath a white vest that exposed her midriff. The toddler was crying and she was trying to comfort him.

How are you my darling?

Fine. So you deemed it fit to visit me today after all this time.

But you were the one who refused to give me a date. Whose child is this?

Mine. Would you adopt him?

Why not? . . . if you'll marry me.

We'll have to wait and see about that.

Can I come in?

No, my family is in and we are not allowed to bring men into the house.

I just want to go in and have a drink of water.

Wait here and I'll bring it to you.

That was the only occasion when Ade Bantan visited Enitan at her family home. It simply was not allowed. Eventually, they drifted away from each other, found other lovers and other pursuits and life continued.

These were the thoughts that drifted through Ade Bantan's mind as he waited on the couch fifteen years later. Sweat trickled out of his body as he awaited Enitan's return from work. What could be keeping her at the advertsing company where she worked as a copywriter? Was she kissing the boss's arse to keep her job? Was she having dinner with some charming client who couldn't have enough of an eyeful of her cleavage? This was awful. What he had become. He lay bathed in perspiration thinking about the whereabouts of his girlfriend. He lay slowly poisoning himself with a swelling tide of bad faith.

Despite all their troubles, Enitan was the one keeping Ade Bantan alive. What would he do without her and her close-knit family? Enitan had three sisters and one brother. She was the eldest; Sumbo came next. Then came Toscin and Susan. The only male in the family was called Joshua. They were all lovely people and welcomed Ade Bantan as one of the family. It was such a source of warmth to be valued by such people.

Sumbo worked as a cashier at a pharmacy, but she was doing all she could to get into a college. Joshua was already attending a provincial university studying business management. Toscin, who had turned twenty-one recently, had just been admitted to study Yoruba at another provincial university. Susan had just got into secondary school. This was all good news, but the financial burden was enormous. They all depended on Enitan for everything; toiletries, water, and food. Enitan bought everything or else everyone starved and stank. It was as simple as that.

Ade Bantan wondered how Enitan coped. Their mother was too old to work and had retired to their home town in the interior of the country. It was a struggle everyday to scrape together food to eat and find enough water to drink. It was a struggle to get electricity to iron a skirt, to have a bath, to breathe. Everything was a struggle.

Enitan was getting exhausted. She needed a partner who would relieve her of some of her burden. All the men she had met before had eventually left her. Some had left because she was mother hen with far too many chicks to look after. Some had left because her endless struggles had made her tough and rough. Such men had wanted misty-eyed romance; they had wanted a woman whose patient bosom would provide a refuge for them from the harshness of the world. Enitan had no patience for such romanticism. Her being had been forged in crucibles of battle, struggle, paw scars, and bite marks. She had scars everywhere. There were scars on her arms from having a fight with a friend who had accommodated her when she was homeless. There were scars deep within, on her spirit, from the battles she fought to get a little water for her family. For every little comfort she received, there was a scar. Scars were common currency, they were the trophies that littered the dangerous corners of each day.

Enitan's remaining softness of heart was fast receding. She knew that she needed some to keep Ade Bantan from running away as so many of her former lovers had. But she was also very tired. She needed to pretend that all was well, that she was holding up brilliantly on her own, that things weren't too bad, that she still had a little horde of laughter remaining in her, that she didn't give a shit when she really did, that she had the presence of mind to build a middle class façade of respectability. Those were Enitan's main thoughts as she carefully plotted the ways of leading him to the altar. If he truly loved her, then he ought to be prepared to share in carrying her burden. But she wasn't sure if she had the strength and the power of concentration to keep up appearances.

Ade Bantan sensed all this was required of him to be with Enitan, but her burdens were beyond his modest capabilities. He loved all of Enitan's siblings, Sumbo, Joshua, Toscin, and Susan. He loved the tact and unobtrusive skill they exercised to transform him into a patriarch. All that was required of him was to lie in his customary position on the couch where they would bring him food and water at meal times. Sumbo would thank him for eating the food. He found the gratuitous gesture overwhelming. The leftovers on the tray would be removed without him having to shift his body from where it lay on the couch. He was being gently eased into the role of a couch potato. It wasn't such a bad life if one wasn't a glutton.

These were the thoughts in Ade Bantan's mind when Sumbo brought a tray of food, boiled plantain, egg, and spinach. It was healthy, energy-giving fare. It was already dark. Two candles in the living room were lit. Sweat poured from his body. Without having touched his meal, he started to fan himself with an old magazine. As a patriarch, he shouldn't appear to be too much in a hurry to devour his meal. There ought to be a sense of grace and composure about his actions and utterances.

But being a cynical opponent of traditional mores, Ade Bantan found it hard to play the role of father of the house. Fuck that shit. Fuck the old men who legislated it into existence. Fuck the generations after them who continued to observe the injunctions whose antecedents had all been forgotten. Fuck the husband, fuck the wife, fuck the entire family and their fucking values of going to church on Sunday. Rather than swallow the enormous bag of lies, he might has well be a junkie slowly withering away on filthy street corner. In his muddled mind, that would serve as a relief instead of being complicit with the hypocrisy that plagued the lives of millions of victims who really ought to know better. The home was built on a lie, it was sustained with lies, and its inhabitants were buried in lies.

Ade Bantan ignored his tray of food as he continued to try to cool his body with the soggy old magazine. He looked out of the window just above him to see what was happening in the next building. He couldn't see much even though a few candles had been lit. Going by the noises he could hear, different families were making preparations for dinner. Serving spoons were being dropped, knives were hacking away on chopping boards, and kerosene stoves were being prompted to life.

Ade Bantan liked to look through the window at the building next door as a measure of knowing how far he had fallen. He had lied to Enitan that he had some art exhibitions coming up in Germany and Switzerland. She had formed the opinion that they were at the gateway to their mutual success. She prayed he would have a successful exhibition and that doors would open for him. Other exhibitions would occur; he would sell lots of paintings and art work; they would have one leg in Europe and one in Africa. They would live the necessary postmodern bi-continental existence. She would give up her job as a wage-slave and learn a profession such as jewelry design in New York. And then, she would spend her life as a woman of means and leisure. Those were her dreams and he had a prominent role in them.

Ade Bantan had to kickstart those decisive exhibitions in Germany and Switzerland to show the way. Once that had been accomplished, she would step in and play her role. She would forget about the exhaustion eating away at her spirit. She would no longer agonize about buying soap, toothpaste, and bread. She would longer have heart palpitations over payment for school fees and medical expenses. Mornings, she would wake up on large king-sized beds with white gleaming sheets. She would spend different seasons in different cities of the world. She would stand triumphant on the dazzling precipice of sight.

Enitan's dreams troubled Ade Bantan. In reality, he had no exhibitions coming up in Germany and Switzerland. He had not produced a single work of art for many years. He had begun to doubt if he had any talent at all. He felt disconnected from himself. He was undergoing a psychological crisis and linking up again with Enitan was meant to serve as an avenue for curing himself of his grave emotional turmoil. He was running out of money but he didn't tell her the true state of things. He was depressed to think that at his age, he did not have a definite direction in life. All his expectations about life and his career had been dashed. He needed some time and space to figure out what to do next.

Enitan's aura had always been able to dispel his innate gloom. She was a healer who didn't realize the immense powers she had over him. She was a medicine woman with a gift she did not know. Ade Bantan had come to her to receive the potent strength of her gift. He had not envisaged that she would have so many familial responsibilities. He would have been ready to remain with her if she hadn't such a heavy load to bear. After she had cured him, he would content himself with light issues. He would spend his days maintaining his health and puttering about the house while she worked.

On days when he felt up to it, he promised himself that he would paint. Perhaps, in time, he would have gathered enough work to mount an exhibition or at least take part in a group exhibition.

Ade Bantan had never really liked solo exhibitions. It placed too much attention on him; the critics had more room to be devastating. They would have precise ideas about what his next step as an artist should be. They would point him in directions he had no wish to go. They would enunciate programs of action to serve as guides for subsequent career moves. He was not interested in all that bullshit. He just wanted to sit on his arse and chat with his adopted family.

Remaining connected with his family meant more to him than a thousand art exhibitions that would only serve as a foil for critics' scribal dross. Perhaps the life of a painter wasn't meant for him. His inner crises had created severe gaps in his state of consciousness and he was unable as at yet to bridge the divisions. He didn't have the power of concentration to focus on producing new work; he had long lost the discipline of diligent application.

With this knowledge in mind, it was difficult to see how he might make any headway as an artist. He knew he couldn't reveal his severe personal doubts and limitations to Enitan. If he did, she would merely throw him out. She had taken him in because she thought he had great potential to be the bearer of an illuminating expanse of hope, the patriarch she had always yearned to have ever since her childhood. It would have been vile of him to destroy her illusions without prior warning. She would never forgive him if he trampled upon the space of her expectations like a gauche ram. Although both Ade Bantan and Enitan needed each other, they were connected in a profound way by a tissue of lies.

Uncle aren't you going to eat your meal? It is already cold, said Sumbo.

Thank you my dear I was only thinking.

You artists think too much. Are you thinking of your next painting?

Not really.

Do you want me to heat up some food for you?

No my dear. It is all right. I will be fine.

Please eat and stop thinking too much.

Ade Bantan knew he had to eat. The meal was healthy and he had to keep up his energy. He began with the spinach and the eggs. It was difficult eating the boiled plantain, since it had gotten cold and hard. He took two bites and left the rest. If he ate more, he would get constipated. Nowadays, he got easily constipated because he did hardly any exercise. All he did all day was lie on the couch watching television or listening to radio. The only real physical activity he engaged in was fucking Enitan before she went to work and when she returned. It was still something. Sumbo came into the room from the passage.

Uncle you've hardly touched the plantain. Are you sick again?

No my dear, I'm not just hungry.

Are you sure you don't want me to reheat the plantain?

I'm just fine. Really, I'm ok.

So I can take the tray to the kitchen then?

Yes my dear. I'm fine.

Thank you uncle for eating a little. We really appreciate it.

It was a pleasure my dear.

These gestures were repeated at every meal time. The father of the house is served a tray of food. He honors the house by eating. The house expresses its gratitude for receiving the father's grace.

Ade Bantan was amazed by the seductive power of patriarchy. He didn't want any part of that kind of shit but his adopted family had introduced him to it and was demonstrating to him its various perks and powers. He was reminded of television programs about wild life, which explored the position of the dominant male lion as the undisputed king of the pride. The king lies in his territory of grassland all day long enjoying the warmth of the sun. At night, his pride of lionesses venture forth in search of buffalo, wildebeest, giraffe, and zebra, which are mauled and killed. At the scent of the kill, the king appears and inaugurates the feast. No feast is approved without the blessing of the king. A feast needed the anointment of the king and this moral is most evident in the depths of the jungle.

Ade Bantan's adopted family had crowned him king and intended him to remain so even though this sometimes made him uncomfortable. If he rejected the role in a brazen manner, he would be not only be spitting upon the hospitality offered by his adopted family, but he would also be violating the law of man and beast. He knew this much even if he didn't agree with the implications of that order of nature. In some secret societies, a king who scorns the throne of monarchy is immediately beheaded. It was regarded as a social disease to refuse to lead or to reject the role of follower. One had to rule or be ruled. The middle ground between the two polarities could only be occupied by fifth columnists, outcasts, and the mentally insane. It is a not a territory that normal creatures inhabit. And so, for the sanity and the purity of the community, people who chose to occupy the non-descript space at the margins of society are banished with the curse of toil-filled death and if the marginalized are kings, they would be put to the sword or beheaded. This knowledge flowed for several centuries in the genes of humankind until its origins became obscured.

By the time Enitan returned from work, everyone was asleep except for Ade Bantan, who only pretended to be. A few nights ago, when she returned from work and Ade Bantan was pretending to be asleep, she had tip-toed over, unloosed the wrap around her body, and exposed her firm gorgeous breasts. He pulled her down and gave her a deep, long kiss. Minutes later, they were having sex on the floor. This night, Enitan went into the inner bedroom and removed all of her clothes, grabbed a multi-colored bedsheet, and returned to the living room to lie on the floor. She did not come to give him a kiss as she had done before.

Ade Bantan and Enitan slept in the living room, while Sumbo, Toscin, and Susan slept in the only available bedroom. It was an extremely small apartment. They had to share communal kitchens, toilets, and baths. And it wasn't a particularly large building, a single story with about eighteen families. Sometimes it was tough having a bath in the morning. There were queues to get a bath, queues to take a shit, queues to warm up a pot of soup. After school, the children ran along the two corridors—one on the ground floor and the other on the first floor—playing games of hide and seek. The yard had no garden or even a blade of grass. The children had to play their games in congested passages of concrete. At the front of the building, Mama Florence stood all day weaving the hair of her clients.

A few blocks to the left, a large white garment church chimed with activity morning and night. Men and women in white flocks without shoes went in and out of the church all day long. Christian hymns were sung at all hours of the day. The hymns were not sung to the accompaniment of electric organs and piano, but sung instead to the sound of tribal drums and loud hand clapping. Half-mad prophets without shoes warned about the imminence of the apocalypse. Witches guilty of murder and blood rites confessed to their sins. Children, whose bodies and souls had been captured by evil beings and forces, were set free.

Strange things happened all the time at the church. Once, a prophet claimed that he had a vision in which the church stood on a ground above a queen serpent that lay coiled on a throne of dark green waters. The prophet demanded the destruction of the church building and a collective cleansing with baptismal waters and fire. The leaders of the church pulled him aside and confided that truly, indeed, a queen serpent did live beneath the church and that it was from there they derived their powers. They explained that if the church were destroyed and the serpent killed, however, then there would be no more congregation. It would spell the end of their mode of worship.

The prophet cried out that they were murderers and that their employment of the word was based on deception, magic, and murder. The leaders of the church replied that power was power, no matter the source.

The prophet reminded them of the distinction between good and evil. He mentioned that the entire structure of the universe was based on an everlasting tussle between the forces of light and darkness, between the angel of light and the black half-man-half-beast who held a fork of blazing coals with a burning intent to rule the world. They told him they weren't children and that he shouldn't preach to them. The prophet replied that all of what he said was based on revelations from the Bible. He then asked them if they were now about to reject the teachings of the holy book. The leaders told him to shut up. The prophet refused and threatened to expose the church as an edifice built on deceit. In turn, the leaders threatened to put a curse on him, in which case he would become insane and wander around the edges of the city talking to plants and trees.

The prophet reminded them that he had walked in the valley of evil, that he had lost his family in the pursuit of truth, that the evil faces of perverted gales accompanied him on the nights that he delivered free sermons; he had power over fear and death, he sat on the right side of the holy throne; he was anointed; in fact, he was the chosen one. The leaders of the church told him they had had enough of this nonsense and threw him out into the streets.

The dreadlocks of the prophet swung into an upheaval of rejection and recrimination. Instead of wandering on the outskirts of the city delivering his sermons to plants and trees, the prophet went about the central districts of the city delivering blistering sermons on the evil of water serpents who reigned beneath church buildings. He gave his sermons facing tone-deaf electric poles.

No one from Enitan's street worshipped at the church above the water serpent. Except the prophet who barked up electric poles about the evil of water serpents, no one was bold enough to warn unsuspecting people of the danger beneath the church. There was a rumor that anyone who dared to disclose the truth about the church would be stricken with blindness and insanity.

Enitan was lying on the floor. Ade Bantan was on the couch trying to ease into sleep amid the cacophony of tribal drums, Christian singing, and hand clapping. Apart from the noise, the heat made it difficult to sleep. In the entire area, buildings stood very close to each other; the numerous illegal

28

electric connections caused a mess of wires around buildings; generators grumbled and farted at all hours; interminable traffic jams created a permanent haze of carbon monoxide fumes; commercial motorcycle riders criss-crossed crater-littered streets trying to avoid instant death while they chased after money; cops worried about how they would make up their quota of bribes; mortuaries groaned from the weight of the dead; medical doctors schemed to become chartered accountants; street urchins held conferences on new ways to extort money; the ocean vomited coins and cowries delivered by innumerable supplicants on the jolting coasts of West Africa; the streams turned brown and fetid with human waste and dead bodies; hope went around in robes of resplendent colors murdering those who offered prayers to it. Days turned into months, months into years, and the laughter of the dead created earthquakes across the land.

The heat continued to suffocate Ade Bantan. He hoped they would get a spurt of electricity for an hour or two. That would be some relief. From the bedroom, different sounds of snoring escaped. Enitan seemed to be fast asleep. Ade Bantan wondered how anyone could sleep with the heat. The old magazine he was using to fan himself had become crumpled and soaked with perspiration. He placed a foot on the window ledge to catch any possible draft. None was to be had. There was a wetness in his crotch. He wondered if he should take his shorts off, and then thought the better of it because he might fall asleep at the crack of dawn and the girls would wake up to see him stark naked. That would be some sight. Personally he couldn't give a fuck, but Enitan would die of embarrassment. What cheek! How could a penis that was meant to be hers alone be shared with the rest of the world like some unappreciated gift from a total mad man? She would rather have the penis chewed up by a pack of stray dogs. Abomination. Would wonders never end? The penis of her man on such public display? Over her dead body!

And so, Ade Bantan continued to endure the disagreeable heat. He would put one leg on the ledge and then put it down again. He would fan himself vehemently with the old mag and then fling it to the floor. Fanning himself wasn't really working. The air was hot and humid. Would it remain this way until dawn? At dawn, the whole neighborhood buzzed with activity. Children going to school, cars blocking up the streets and innumerable wage-slaves going to usher in the ceremony of the dead at various corporate offices. Those who didn't have the fortune to be slaves remained at home with the unpaid task of tending the gates of the dead. It was the age of the universal reign of the dead. The dead went into death-filled streets everyday and into the houses of the dead. At home, they left behind unemployed battalions of the dead who manned the gates of the dead. It was one endless cycle of death feeding upon itself beginning from its own head and down to its tail. Between the dead who toiled as slaves and the dead who remained at home to man the gates lay the great deception. The deception that claimed that there was a fundamental difference between the two. It was bullshit straight-up. It was the swindle of the millennium.

But of what use was this kind of knowledge? Could he disclose his thinking to Enitan, or Sumbo, or Toscin? Of course not. They would think he had lost his mind. They would hurl him to a redemption camp and ask for deliverance on his behalf. They'd have him whipped and kicked into shape by soldiers at the camp. They would rip off his clothes and clamp him in chains. They would douse him with buckets of holy water until he almost drowned. They would throw him into dungeons where the spiritually afflicted souls muttered about incomprehensible visions and told tales of madness and incest among church brethren. No, he dared not speak his mind about his terrible knowledge. If he did, he would be an uncivilized destroyer of illusions and entrenched societal orders.

What was the point? He didn't have the strength to convey the implications of his knowledge. He hadn't the gift of communication by which to pronounce the abominable. He didn't possess a prophet's concentration of vision and madness to bark against lifeless edifices. His cloud preferred to drift in quieter zones where marijuana fumes told you to take it easy and that all would be well. His sight landed on heroin addicts in a state of protracted chill-out as they hovered on the grey borders of consciousness. His cloud alluded to states of being in which folds of consciousness collapsed inward to become a soft mash of wind, water, and white sands. So, as the harsh sunlight gained even more strength, Ade Bantan's heart shed tears no one could see.

The heat had not subsided. The rage of hand clapping and tribal drums continued. The hours ticked away slowly. Ade Bantan ambled to the balcony in the front of the building. He felt slightly better as he leaned against the railings and held out his face to catch some coolness. He always sauntered to the balcony anytime the heat in the small apartment became unbearable. It helped in some ways. But he also feared that he might see a band of armed robbers invade the streets and start an operation.

The building was located in a close and the path leading to the dead-end was quite short. All robbers had to do was block up the exits while they conducted a systematic raid on all the buildings of the street. This was a common occurrence in the neighborhood. If an operation started while he was on the balcony catching some breeze, then he was fucked. They would call him down and force him to be their guide. They would ask him to provide information regarding the all the occupants of the building. If he failed to provide accurate information, as many as twenty men might take turns sodomizing him. Or, they might gang-rape Enitan and her sisters as a means of revenge. This was why he was not always comfortable hanging out on the balcony after midnight.

The heat and mosquitoes tormented indoors. Heartbreak, suffering, and horror threatened outdoors. They were a threshold where occult masqueraders stalked the land and traumatized those unfortunate to see them. Time spent outdoors after midnight was for the migration of vultures and crows with decaying human flesh on their beaks. Time spent outside was meant for occultists who feed vehicular crossroads with bowls of offerings to finish off the faint-hearted and those that lack knowledge. After midnight, there was always a cornucopia for those hungry and willing to watch for the night's arse to take a shit. Night laughs at them whose eyes are untrained and unchained, for they will be banished into the kingdom that lies between the land of the half dead and the ocean of the dead. For sustanance, they would suck at the marrows in the bones of the dead. Their lungs burn at every inhalation of dead air. For comfort they can only turn toward gusts of blazing heat.

The elders on Enitan's street warned that the night time was the worst because it was the junction where the evils of men and the dark wrath of the gods met. Night was not the time for the innocent to stroll. Night was the time for a dance of dark blood in cold twisted street corners.

Ade Bantan had had enough of the breeze, so he returned inside to the whining of mosquitoes and the suffocating heat. How did he get himself into a life of such ruthless extremes? How long could he keep up the façade of going to sleep each night with such relentless horrors? He needed Enitan to provide structure to his days. He needed her to get him out of himself and maintain a link to the world. He needed her to enjoy the light of laughter and easy days. He needed her to get from one day to the next.

The snores in the bedroom kept droning. Enitan hadn't shifted from where she lay. Ade Bantan walked gingerly to couch and lay. He put his leg and the ledge and tried to force himself to sleep. The mosquitoes kept buzzing in his ears. Some even strayed into his nostrils. It was hopeless. He pulled himself to the window ledge to see if the skies were lightening up. It seemed dawn was still a few hours away. He had a few more hours to suffer. Slowly the minutes ticked away as he fought away mosquitoes and tried to endure the heat and humidity. A leg on the ledge for a few minutes and then the leg falling off the ledge onto the couch. There was no respite. His body grew tired and in spite of all the annoyances, he managed to grab snatches of sleep.

The sky started to lighten up. A multitude of prayers shook the neighborhood. The racket of tribal drums, Pentecostal singing, and hand clapping had not subsided in the white garment church. Papa Osaze's voice could be heard deep in prayer from the next door. Papa Osaze was a particularly powerful prayer warrior.

The act of prayer in several contemporary Christian denominations was seen as act of war. It was a war against the devil. It was a war against the temptations of the flesh. It was a war against adultery. It was a war against fornication. It was a war against lying. It was a war against covetousness. It was a war against deception. It was a war against disease. It was a war against blindness. It was a war against deafness. It was a war against stroke. It was a war against alcoholism. It was war against drug abuse. It was a war against pagans. It was a war against Muslims. It was a war against adherents of occultism. It was a war against magic. It was a war against the lack of faith. It was a war against unChristian fundamentalisms. It was a war against terror. It was a war against all those who waged wars that were not sanctioned as holy. It was a war against the roving eye. It was a war against the inconstant heart. It was a war against unholy books. It was a war against television. It was a war against wristwatches. It was a war against earrings. It was a war against permed hair. It was a war against mascara and make up. It was a war against females wearing trousers. It was a war against men who slept with men. It was a war against lesbians. It was a war against men who had sex with dogs, horses, or donkeys. It was a war against traditional healers. It was a war against purveyors of the herb. It was a war against witches and wizards. It was a war against black birds that crowed at night. It was a war against black cats that meowed at the stroke of midnight and no other time. It was a war against those who made trouble for the holy messengers. It was a war against pretenders. It was an outright war against everything that stood of the path of the holy. Lo, let it be known that the mighty sword would fall upon those that stand in the way of the word's progress. In the march of victory none shall stand in the way of the word.

Papa Osaze believed all of this to be true. None should stand in the way of the word. Those who do shall be mercilessly struck down with vengeance. Due to the diligence and vehemence of Papa Osaze's prayers, he became the unofficial religious leader of the yard. Married couples with marital problems would seek his guidance and advice. Parents with errant teenagers would consult him about how to bring them in line.

To make ends meet, Papa Osaze worked as a motor mechanic. He had four kids: Osaze aged eleven; Angel, nine; Amber, six; and Blessing, who was eight months old. His overweight wife was called Mama Osaze. Enitan loved Blessing and would always accept a request to babysit for her when her mother was busy cooking or doing some minor shopping nearby.

Everyone in the yard loved Blessing and other children in the yard who were younger than one year old. Such children were carried by everyone and smothered with care and kisses. It would be perhaps the only time in their lives that they would enjoy such attention. Once they were more than four years old, they would be taught to fetch water, run across the streets to buy condiments for a meal, hop over open sewers to get water to drink, buy cigarettes and beer for uncles, carry babies across murky gutters when their mothers were away, and do countless other errands. They also had to find some elusive space to finish their school homework. It was not easy to find such a space. The white garment church chimed with continual singing and drumming. The commercial motorcycle riders hooted through the streets. Peddlers of pap, sugar, tea, bread, fresh fish, meat, and cassava shouted all day promoting their wares. Fights broke out between husband and wife, distracting everyone's attention. Neighbors picked quarrels about whose turn it was to clean up the kitchen or the toilet. Clothes went missing on the clothing lines and heated conferences were organized to deliberate on new security measures. The problems of the yard and the commotion of the street clogged up the head spaces of adults and children alike.

The mess of electric wires above produced their own peculiar tension. The earth beneath simmered with man-made artificial heat. Everyone shrank from the heat. This was why the likes of Papa Osaze prospered. People like him returned fire with fire. They devoured fire-emitting dragons with the fire of the word. They did battle with fire in both the literal and metaphysical sense. The spirit of fire was reduced in their presence because they themselves had become fire. When faced with the terror of fire, people like Papa Osaze did not employ the soothing ministrations of water, earth, or air. Instead, they emitted a mix of fumes and fury to attack invading flames of fire. They proclaimed the reign of fire throughout the land. Fire on the water. Fire upon the land. Fire in the winds. Fire on the mountain. When such fires appeared, people like him knew it a sign of the impending apocalypse. It was a time of angels with swords of fire. It was a time when all visions and dreams of fire, of spiritual cleansing, of the anointing, and of more fire are fulfilled. If the foundation of evil is fire, then fire shall provide the basis for the cleansing.

Such was the spiritual thinking of people like Papa Osaze. This was the basis upon which he claimed the title of prayer warrior. Prayer warriors were messengers of fire. They argued that the secret of fire does not reside with a chosen few. The secret of fire can be found on earth, in the winds, on the peaks of mountains, and within the seas. The mystery of fire reveals itself for itself and for others. It has a dual way of walking forwards and backwards at the same time. The secret of fire can be found everywhere. One only has to study the hysterical dances and contortions of the flames. One has to follow the neuroses of red maidens as they rend trees with barking noises and draw scars of light across the breast of the sky.

Papa Osaze was the first to commence morning devotion in the yard and the last to finish. Ade Bantan was not sure whether he could catch a mere two hours of sleep on any given night. How could he, with prayer warriors launching attacks from all sides? Susan had already been awakened by Sumbo to prepare for school. She was a sweet, conscientious girl who did as she was told. Each morning after waking, she would go to the bowl at the edge of the bedroom where toothbrushes, paste, and soap were kept, and then repair to the bathroom. A light brown towel was tied around her chest. Her breasts had yet to bud, but she was good looking and had a pleasant disposition. She didn't talk to elders except when necessary. She stayed away from the more dangerous games that kids of the yard played. After school, a private teacher arranged by Enitan came to tutor her in English and mathematics because she was a barely average student and needed extra studies to get by.

Sumbo came to the living room to sweep, as she did almost every day except on occasions Toscin decided to do it. Enitan went into the bedroom to get some more sleep on the mattress that lay on the floor. Ade Bantan joined her in order to give Sumbo room to do her chores. Sumbo made sure the living room was clean because it was a busy meeting point. Neighbors came for daily bouts of chit chat; friends strolled in to crash for the night; relatives came and went as they wished; children of all ages ran in and out. It was necessary to keep getting rid of the dust many feet kept bringing in. Sumbo made it her task to do so. The bright red carpet had to be kept clean because she and Enitan loved to lie on it.

Indeed, almost everyone, adults and children alike, loved to lie on the bright red carpet in the room that gave the apartment a striking singularity. The walls were painted a dull green. There were a stereo and a television set on a cabinet near the door. There were a couch and two upright chairs. That was about it. A struggling professional's pad. But everyone was relatively happy with the small comforts. The carpet was there for all to lie on; they could listen to music and watch movies together from time to time. Many friends came around for some fun. Life was awfully tough, but they could still afford to wear a smile. This was the quality that most baffled Ade Bantan about Enitan's siblings. He would never forget the charming brilliance and heartfelt warmth of Toscin's smile when he was first welcomed to their home. Enitan had not returned from work. Neither had Sumbo. He arrived at about a quarter past seven in the evening. Toscin looked like a professional model, tall, elegant, and graceful with a fair complexion. On that evening, she wore a light blue floral shirt over a pair of dark blue jeans. Her hair was braided into corn rows. Ade Bantan had gone weak at the knees on account of her beauty.

As the familiar sounds of Sumbo sweeping drifted into the bedroom, Ade Bantan closed his eyes. He thought of ways of catching snatches of forced sleep amid the awakening tides of commotion. It was a futile effort. Two streets away, he could hear construction workers hammering away on steel and concrete. The hooting of vehicles and motorcycles had grown louder. Street vendors were making use of the morning freshness and its energies before the enervating rages of the mid-day sun. He hated it when the sun was at full strength. It filled him with a hopeless sense of ennui. He had nothing to do but swear within himself and give out hot buckets of sweat.

Susan returned from the bathroom with the towel still wrapped around her flat chest. She hadn't noticed that Ade Bantan's eyes were only half-closed when she came in. He shut his eyes a wee bit more. He didn't want her to catch him looking at her because it would make her self-conscious. Susan let the towel slip off her lithe body and stooped to rub some body lotion over herself. For many months, he watched

38

this simple ritual of her moisturising herself and never failed to marvel at its innocence.

Susan was on the precipitous brink between childhood and adolescence in terms of body awareness. She had not yet discovered the full potential of her sensuality. Perhaps it was because she lived predominantly among women. They undressed together and slept on the same mattress. They were her sisters and would do nothing to injure the pace of her individual growth. Ade Bantan was certain that once she discovered him watching her, she would recoil and start to relate more directly to the implications of her evolving sensuality. The discovery of his eyes upon her would create a chain of reactions within the very delicate chemistry that existed between them. He wouldn't have wanted to her to get the impression he was an old lecher. He was a plain and simple uncle who was about to marry her eldest sister.

Ade Bantan was not prepared to engineer or preside over the destruction of these most cherished of impressions. He did not want that to happen, so he ensured that his eyes were almost totally closed as he watched Susan rub lotion on her naked body. Susan pulled a pair of finger-sized panties up her slender thighs, threw her school uniform over her head, put on her shoes, grabbed her school bag, and dashed off to school without having had breakfast. Sumbo threw her a packet of biscuits as she was about to run out of the living room.

Enitan's congested bedroom was a space of surprises. Each and every inch of space mattered. The room contained all the clothing belonging to Enitan, Sumbo, Toscin, and Susan. It also had more than half of Joshua's clothing even though he was away at university. It also had a fair amount of Ade Bantan's clothing. Enitan was particularly enamored of clothes. She bought them everywhere she could find them.

She saved and bought some from exquisite designers. She purchased some from the makeshift stalls of street traders. She bought some from hawkers who sold their wares on wooden boards over sewers. Her love for clothes knew no bounds. He remembered an occasion when she had fallen ill with a bout of malaria and he had taken her to a shabby hospital because it was what they could afford. Once Enitan received her treatment, she was bargaining with a street hawker who was selling a rack of tacky looking clothes at the nearest bus stop. He was in a hurry to get her home to rest, but she wouldn't budge until she bought three blouses from the jumble. He was impressed with her selection. He wondered how she could spot such good pieces from what appeared to be a little forest of shabby second-hand clothes. Simply amazing. On another day, when they had visited yet another congested area of the city, Enitan made them stop on a wooden pedestrian bridge to make a down payment on a few body-hugging tops. Enitan made a deal with the-most-out of-the-way hawker one could imagine.

Making such frequent purchases, Enitan had turned the bedroom into a jungle. Against the wall beside the door, heaps of clothing were mounted haphazardly. Some were clean, but many others were not. Some were squeezed into traveling bags and some were just floating over the mass of everything. Against the wall at the head of the mattress, yet another mountain of clothes was bunched into a corner. Next to this particular mountain, there were two plastic baskets containing plates, plastic containers, jars of condiments, cutlery, and glasses. There was a bowl for toiletries. Behind the door where an old calendar had been pinned, was a small regrigerator in which drinks were kept. Behind the same door, Enitan also kept a collapsible shoe rack that held a fraction of her shoes. The rest were stored amid the jungle of clothes.

Since the women could not hang their panties in the communal bathroom, Enitan hung hers to dry in the bedroom on a string attached to the door. Ade Bantan wasn't sure where Susan hung hers.

Below the only window in the room, Enitan collected her various magazines, CDs, and DVDs. There were also a few self-help and religious books in the same place. The books and magazines sometimes got wet when lashings of rain came in through the window. On the window ledge, Sumbo kept bits and pieces of medicated soap to fight acne, small jars of petroleum jelly, and half-empty tubes of lip gloss. There were also a couple of old toothbrushes and cracked pieces of mirror on the same ledge. Across the window hung a rusty wire mosquito net that had come off the edges.

The only unoccupied place in the bedroom was the mattress. Ade Bantan's gear was stuffed into a bag and tossed beneath the heaps of clothing. He sometimes had trouble locating it. In spite of the mess and lack of space, Enitan designated the bedroom as her haven. Only a few trusted friends were invited in to sit or lie on the mattress. She had become particularly stringent when bundles of her clothing started to go missing. It was easy for bundles of clothing to go missing in such a jungle. Theft went unnoticed for many weeks, or sometimes, months. Enitan would suddenly remember that a particular blouse went with this specific handbag and then initiate a futile search for the blouse. All her sisters joined in her search; the bedroom was turned further upside-down, thereby creating a more confusing jumble.

However, it would be a mistake to think that there was a complete lack of understanding of the mess within which they lived. Sumbo, for one, had a knack of ferreting out a missing shoe, a hidden purse or comb, or even a concealed make-up kit. After all, she cleaned the room. The jumble of the room also had an elaborate metaphorical relation. It signified the connectedness of everyone in the apartment to one another. Each and everyone's clothes contributed to the jungle, and in that sense, created a seamless relation of unity. Space was not individualized and threatened by a foreign conceptualization of privacy. Instead, space was deployed as an entity to further the aims of bondedness and communality over the violence of difference and separateness. Enitan had provided the blueprint for the strategy by undertaking to act as a mother hen. Sumbo was the efficient tactician, who implemented the requirements of the overall strategy. She enforced the day-to-day framework by which the nuts and bolts would be effective. Everything had been put in place and the rest had only to follow.

Ade Bantan sensed that a specific conception of togetherness was being enacted. What he did not immediately observe was the depth of that conception. Indeed, the notion of family aspires to an overarching ideal of blood-based unity. But it is also an ideal that is infrequently realized and often prone to abuse. Enitan's experience of familial abuse and betrayal had led her to a strict policy of overcompensation. Apart from this policy of overcompensation, the necessity for survival demanded an uncompromising unity of purpose. In this regard, Enitan and Sumbo were as one. They would be sisters for life. They would be there for each other through thick and thin. Ade Bantan found their sense of unity admirable. His heart grew heavy with yearning any time he thought about it. But he also had to start thinking about how his inclusion into this well-crafted strategy would play out. Enitan had presented the strategy as a *fait accompli*. There was no argument, no contestation, and hence, no change in strategic policy. He found that stance difficult to cope with.

No change in strategic policy? How would they meet all their material needs? How would they continue to get by from day-to-day? Enitan had hinted in unambiguous ways that she wanted to visit the altar of marriage with him. He now faced two major problems in his life. How was he to overcome his protracted bout of artistic drought? How would he marry Enitan without managing to destroy the unity of her family? For now he had no answers to these questions.

Ade Bantan continued to watch Enitan as she slept. She usually left for work at eight thirty, and it was only seven thirty. He would need to wake her up at quarter to eight so she could have a bath, put on her make-up, and perhaps have a bite if there was any time left. It was regarded as his duty to get her out of bed on time each morning. He didn't mind; after all, what else was he doing? He had the entire day at his disposal and the sad truth was that he didn't know what to do with his time. He spent most of his time going from one welcoming cigarette shed to the other, smoking cigarettes. He didn't like to smoke in the yard because of the children. There weren't many places to smoke in the neighborhood. School compounds were under lock and key after school hours. Cigarette kiosks jostled dangerously with barber shops atop sewers. Internet cafés took space up to the lip of the streets. It was too hot to hang out in beer bars at midday. Pedestrians trampled through crooked and narrow pathways all day long. Motorcyclists took up the margins between sewers and the streets. Hairdresser shops and call centers made the area even more congested. Hawkers carrying trays of wares on their heads threatened to shove off both pedestrians and motorcyclists. Garbage took up the space between sewers and the streets. Churches and mosques jutted out of narrow alleyways. Makeshift markets selling tomatoes, onions, meat, yam, cassava, and plantain occupied spaces that had not been taken up by cheap liquor sellers and barbers who worked underneath trampoline. Supposedly vacant spaces had been taken up by sewerage, rubbish, and mud. Flies buzzed about the little pieces of waste. There was no space to do anything. There was no space for a cigarette outdoors, no space for thieves to run, no grounds for chickens to forage, no space for a pee or a shit.

But there was some space for the odd jet of spit. The neighborhood chewed up its inhabitants and then ruthlessly spat them out because it had no space to keep them. Some slept on balconies. Some sleep in corridors. Some slept underneath tables. Some slept inside kitchens. Some slept in courtyards. Some slept from room-to-room. Some slept with friends. Some slept with enemies. Some slept in bus conductors' rooms. Some others slept in bus stations. Some slept where they could be eaten alive. Some others slept where they could eat people alive. Some slept in churches and some others slept in mosques. It was a miracle how anyone managed to get some sleep with all the heat, mosquitoes, and endless commotion. Were there more lies than truth about the realities of sleeping? Was the pretext of sleeping a camouflage for an acute lack of it? People are meant to sleep, so sleep they should. But was this really possible? This was something Ade Bantan wished he could discover.

Enitan was still sleeping with her legs apart and her face squashed against the pillow. It was time to wake her up. He shook her by the shoulder gently until she opened her eyes. The wonders of awakening were slowly making their way into her fuzzy brain.

What time is it darling?

Oh, its only quarter to eight.

44

Thanks for waking me up darling.

Enitan yawned and scratched her firm right breast. Her upper thighs were exposed. Ade Bantan felt the throb of a bulge in his shorts. He had wanted to get himself a glass of water but he now had to wait until the bulge disappeared. Sumbo or Toscin could come in any time.

So what are you doing to today?

The usual. Have breakfast, take my shower, and then walk around the area at sunset waiting for inspiration. I really ought to start preparing for my exhibitions in Germany and Switzerland.

Yeah you should. I would love to visit those countries and see what opportunities are available. You must try and produce your best work. Create a forceful impression and see where it leads you.

You bet I will.

I trust you darling. Come here, give me a kiss.

They smacked lips.

Thank you my darling. Would you like me to get you anything on my way back from work?

No my love, I'm fine.

Are you sure? You never seem to want anything. Are you feeling shy to ask?

How can I be? If I need anything darling I will let you know.

Good. Always remember that I am here for you.

Enitan stood up from the mattress and tied a wrap around her. She also tied a multi-colored shawl around her head. She looked gorgeous as the bulge in Ade Bantan's shorts confirmed. He couldn't understand why she taking such a beautiful shawl to the bathroom. What sort of statement could she be making early in the morning? Enitan appeared to be on an unspoken mission to prove that she was the coolest woman in the yard, on the street, and perhaps the entire neighborhood.

You look beautiful darling.

Thank you my love.

Would you need an escort to the bathroom?

I always need an escort my love.

Great, I'll go with you.

Enitan made her way to the bathroom with Ade Bantan trailing her a meter and a half behind. The folks who lived in the apartment facing Papa Osaze were awake. Papa Osaze had taken his children to school on the way to his place of work. Blessing could be heard crying. Apart from Enitan and Ade Bantan, no one else was in the corridor. For Ade Bantan, that was wonderful. It meant that he could enter the bathroom with Enitan unnoticed. The corridor led to a partially roofed courtyard. Across the void, there were clotheslines hanging overhead with a few items of clothing. On the right, there was a line of doors opening up to baths and toilets. Beyond the line of doors to the left was the communal kitchen for all the occupants of the floor. It was where Enitan's family made their meals. Enitan ducked through the door meant for her apartment. It was always open, unlike some others which were kept shut when not in use.

Enitan left the door unlocked. Looking to the right and left, Ade Bantan slipped in. Enitan turned on the tap to fill a light green plastic bucket with water. Ade Bantan pulled the single wooden window in the bathroom partially shut. It was best to do so because they were visible from the next building. The building had a small chalet on the side, which had a rusty roof of corrugated iron. One could see it distinctly through the bathroom window. It had all manner of rubbish on it; old coins, rubber balls, bicycle tires, heads and limbs of Barbie dolls, torn shoes. Occupants on the first floor of the main building could also see them. But it was difficult to see if they were being watched because some of the rooms were in darkness. Through one of the windows, Ade Bantan could just make out a light green wall with a large calendar, the back of a chair, and the end of a table. He could see nothing more from the angle at which he stood. The floor of the bathroom was slippery with muck and grime. Gently, he went down on Enitan, placing one of her legs over his shoulders. He thrust his tongue between her thighs and began to lick her clit. Enitan wriggled with pleasure. She shut her eyes and her head fell backwards. She was determined to embark on a journey to nirvana. He was determined to pilot her there. She placed one arm on the window ledge and the other on Ade Bantan's shoulder to maintain her balance. She started moan softly and then more audibly.

Ade Bantan eyes kept flitting to the black key hole after a few moments. He knew there were peeping toms in yard who sometimes spied upon couples in their intimate sessions behind closed doors. In the past, a tenant of sixty-five, Papa Jumbo, had moaned audibly while making love to his young wife of twenty-four, and had been heard by a prankish young man who then called other tenants to come and listen by the door. Afterwards, each time Papa Jumbo walked pass, the tenants who had listened by his door would moan, mimicking him. Fed up with their taunts and out of embarrassment, Papa Jumbo and his young wife moved out of the premises to an even more decrepit building six streets away. That was the only way he could gain some peace of mind.

When Ade Bantan put Enitan's leg down gently on the slippery floor, her eyes were glazed from deep pleasure. He was pleased. He pulled off his shorts and turned her toward the window ledge, which she grabbed for support. They had kept the water running to conceal the sounds of their love making. She was wet when he entered her from behind. Her head jerked at every thrust he made. After a couple of minutes, he had an explosive orgasm. His own moans exceeded Enitan's in volume. She cautioned him a few times to be quiet. He couldn't help himself as he shook from head to toe. They had gotten through one of their more pleasurable rituals.

Go on now darling I've got to have a bath.

Ade Bantan leaned against the walls with his arms as he gradually recovered his senses. He couldn't move just yet because he could fall. He gave a huge sigh of relief when he was finally ready to leave the bathroom. He grabbed his shorts from where they hung on a string that ran from the top of the door to the window. He pulled them up his thighs and whispered to Enitan to look out to see if the courtyard was clear. Enitan unlocked the door, peered out, and nodded to him. He could go. He quickly stepped into the courtyard while she re-locked the door. When he got to the corridor, he saw Mama Osaze with Blessing on her back returning to her apartment. She did not turn around to look at him.

Sumbo was dusting the cabinet that housed the stereo and the television set. The bright red carpet looked sparkling as he crossed into the bedroom and slumped on the mattress. His breathing had not yet resumed its normal pace as he closed his eyes and waited to regain full composure. It had been a thoroughly delightful experience.

Enitan usually took about fifteen minutes to finish bathing. By the time she came back into the cramped bedroom, Ade Bantan had fully recovered from their bout of slightly uncomfortable lovemaking. He loved to watch her rub lotion all over her body. He loved to see her pull up her g-string. Perhaps for his benefit, she'd leave off her bra as she proceeded to apply make-up on her face. Her skill in applying make-up came in handy; she had to be functional, time-conscious, and effective all at once. Enitan managed to combine all these qualities in lining her eye-brows with pencil, daubing her cheeks and forehead with powder, and applying lip gloss. She contrived to strike a balance between chic deportment, postmodernity, and efficiency. He could see that she had honed the task to an art form. It was indeed an art. He appreciated the years of work she had put into her art. He also appreciated that she was never self-conscious about him observing her while she went about the task of visually transforming herself with a blend of off-handedness and practiced accuracy.

In relation to Enitan, Ade Bantan's personal hygiene practices were haphazard. He ascribed this to the fact that he despised being the subject of the voyeuristic eye. It was all right for him to be a voyeur, but he couldn't stand being the center of attention. Being the focus of attention threw his feet into his mouth and made him fall into pits and shit. Hence, his lack of a sophisticated personal hygiene routine stemmed from a deep-seated psychological discomfort with ensnaring eyes and cameras. He never wanted to be within their fields of vision.

Enitan, on the other hand, simply couldn't give a damn. Neither the eye nor the camera was powerful enough to disrupt the natural flow of her rhythms. Her rhythms came directly from her own motivations and were not dependent on the promptings and subtle persuasions of the regarding eye. The eye tries to seduce you to do more for it. It attempts to prompt you to lose your inhibitions and bare it all. You are either convinced by this argument and you really do bare it all and become a complete idiot, or you are like a hare caught frozen in the sudden glare of vehicular headlights. Therein lies the power of the camera and the regarding eye. The regarding eye has been an arbiter of the age-long tussle between Apollo and Dionysus. One promotes the virtues of discipline and asceticism, while the other pronounces the gains of excess and freak occurrences of genius. The regarding eye lures an unsuspecting subject between these extremities and begins a silent argument until the subject is compelled to make a decision.

Enitan was ready to leave for work. She had on a pair of dark brown pair slacks that emphasized her generous curves with a see-through blouse with green and brown stripes that loomed like elongated leaves. Beneath her blouse, her black bra was visible. She looked stunning. It was time for Ade Bantan to see her off to the bus station three streets away.

As they made their way to the bus shed, dozens of pairs of eyes followed them. The male eyes looked at them with feelings of appreciation, thwarted emotion, and naked lust. The female eyes largely regarded with them with envy and bigotry. Enitan couldn't care less as the arrogant strut of her bosom continued down the street. The eyes that had lined up for the parade behind filthy curtains, dark doorways, and cracks along walls pined for freedom from Enitan's pitiless reign. They longed for a modicum of acknowledgement and generosity; they yearned to be invited into the warmth, generosity, and community of Enitan's bosom. But Enitan would never give in to their unrealistic desires. She did not do charity. She was a mother hen with lots of chicks of her own to feed.

Ade Bantan looked like Enitan's bodyguard in his bright yellow t-shirt that he always slept in and a pair of skimpy shorts that were equally shabby. Invariably, the eyes regarding Enitan fell upon him. They were curious to know who he was, what he did. Was he sleeping with her? What did she see in him? Doesn't he look like a bum? Is he her bodyguard or mere domestic hand? Could she truly be sleeping with a domestic? he must have a really nice package. Does he do any work at all? Are his performances restricted to the bedroom?

Ade Bantan knew he was bound to generate some amount of interest. You do not walk along with a resplendent peacock and not get noticed. He who dines with the peacock necessarily becomes the subject of the regarding eye. His discomfort with his situation was not something he could easily get used to. It was a small ordeal of torture to walk

Enitan to the bus stop each morning in his threads. It was also an ordeal when he had to walk back alone.

At last, they reached the bus stop and a commercial vehicle swung into a stop beside them. The driver gave Enitan no time to sit properly. Drivers usually never did. Usually they swung into motion while you were still standing as the conductor yelled for more customers. There had been no time for Ade Bantan to brush Enitan's cheeks as he normally did before she entered a bus.

It was now time for Ade Bantan to make his way toward the apartment after being frisked and devoured by unknown eyes. He trembled from the ordeal. He walked slowly, trying not to miss too many steps, exhibiting his nervousness. Cars passed, hawkers with baskets of pap and sugar-cane on their heads screamed as they went by, school children in different uniforms sauntered past in droves. He passed stalls selling tomatoes, red pepper, onions, fish, and meat. He passed by mosques that were a story high, and then he was almost struck by a commercial motorcycle rider. It jerked away from him just as it was about to crush his leg. He grew even more nervous as a result of his lucky escape. He needed a cigarette badly to recover his wits. He needed to find a kiosk where he could sit and think. He loved to smoke hidden from the harsh sunlight, but it was difficult to find places that had sufficient space and shade. He had to walk for about a kilometer to find a suitable joint. All the kiosks had been mounted in front of houses that barely had any space left, or on the ground between the houses and the street, or above open sewers, or in narrow pedestrian alleys. There was virtually no space anywhere. Every available inch had been taken up by stalls that folded up all the time to be replaced by new ones. There was no place to sit and have a smoke underneath some makeshift shed. There was no place to cough. All the trees had been chopped down to make way for roads, houses, and more kiosks. There was no protection from the glare of the sun. The birds had disappeared and the lizards were dying out. People who had nightmares about eating human beings sought refuge in churches. There were half a dozen churches in every street. The sun spat out its ire in disgust at the lack of space and solitude.

Ade Bantan returned to Enitan's apartment. In the corridor, he met Chidi, who lived with his mother and three sisters in the apartment opposite Papa Osaze's. Chidi went from one Internet café to another in the neighborhood trying to learn all kinds of computer skills because he couldn't afford a computer of his own. He sometimes came to use Enitan's laptop when it was available. Although he had a pleasant disposition, he was fairly desperate. His mother had been thrown out of the job market and he relied mainly on two of his sisters, who worked, for material support. His third sister was a religious fanatic who prayed loudly all day by herself. Chidi's father had abandoned the family when his business went bankrupt. They recently learned that he had taken a new wife and had settled back in his hometown. Chidi couldn't wait to leave his mother and sisters. He felt oppressed by all of them. He could never do right by them. His mother blamed him for everything. She told him he was lazy and heckled him constantly to get a job. But how could he get a good job when he had no qualifications?

Chidi begged his sisters to give him money for computer parts so that he could at least put one together himself. They jeered at him and told him he was wasting his time. None of them believed he would amount to anything. They insulted him, saying that he ate too much, that he consumed more than he could ever afford in his life. In order to avoid their constant taunts, he would go without food for days on end and sometimes fell ill. Ill health did not prevent his family from jeering at him. It got to be so much for him that he started sleeping on the balcony of his apartment at the mercy of the night chill and mosquitoes. He prayed constantly for an opportunity to leave his family for good. He prayed for his own little corner on earth where he could take in some air. He prayed for a bit of silence in his life. He prayed for a respite from the insults and jeers. He prayed to own an old computer of his own. He prayed for a girlfriend who would understand. He prayed for things to go well sometimes in his life. He prayed for a bit of good fortune.

Hi bro. How goes it?

I'm great Chidi and you?

It's not easy bro. The same old shit. The same old shit never changes.

Continue to pray.

I pray every single day bro. No luck yet. Maybe I should start attending church more seriously.

Maybe you should.

It's not easy bro. I don't even have good clothes to wear to church.

You don't need fine clothes to attend church.

I don't even have money for my transport fare.

How about your sisters?

Forget about them. They're no good.

But they feed and accommodate you.

Bro, you don't know how bad they are.

They treat me worst than a dog.

You don't meant that.

I do bro! They kick the living shit out of me. They have no mercy for me.

It can be that bad.

It is much worse than you think or could ever know. Just because I keep everything to myself doesn't mean that it isn't bad. Please don't let anyone know what I am telling you. Those devils would kill me dead if they knew.

Of course you know whatever we say stays between us. Mum's the word.

Bro, is Aunty Enitan's computer free?

No, she took it with her to the office.

Tough luck. Perhaps I should come and listen to music with you for a short while.

No problem at all. You know you're always welcome.

Ade Bantan loved Chidi's company. They had something in common. They were both stuck in their lives and were in desperate need of a change of direction. To cover up the gnawing emptiness in their lives, they gossiped. Chidi used to have a girlfriend who lived in an apartment at the back with her mother, but she dumped him once she entered the university. She felt he wasn't getting anywhere professionally and didn't have a penny to his name. This further devastated him. Ade Bantan seemed to be the only one who continued to have some confidence in him. When they settled into the living room to talk, Sumbo was getting ready for work. Toscin had gone out to pick up some groceries and satchels of drinking water. Water had to be bought. Water directly from the tap meant typhoid. He settled in his customary position on the couch. Chidi lay on the floor trying to find new rumors to spread.

Have you heard that the woman who lives opposite my former girlfriend has tested positive for the virus?

Oh come on; that's a lie.

Of course it's true. How could someone lie about such a thing?

Who told you?

I was sitting in front of the yard one evening and this guy comes asking for Mama Lizzy. I ask him what for, and he says he's got some anti-retrovirals for her.

Did you take him to her?

Yeah I did. Can't you see how much she's changed?

What spectacular changes have you noticed?

For one, she's lost all her hair and wears a wig permanently.

Is that all?

Her lips are also always white and she always seems to be exhausted.

You had better keep this to yourself.

You're the only one I discuss such things with in this yard. God, I can't stand the people in compound. They are all hypocrites. Worthless busybodies who keep sticking their noses in other people's business. We ought to get a couple of thugs to break a few noses and then perhaps we might see a change of attitude. And they're so envious. If you put on a new shirt, they want to know how you got it, how much it cost, where you got it, and so on and so forth. They never want to see you do well so that they can always find something bad to laugh about.

Well it is a pity.

It really is. There isn't a single man in this compound that has any balls. Their wives are completely in charge. They stick their husbands' heads between their thighs and give them a good spanking. The men would be wailing like babies if not for their embarrassment. You hardly see them at all. They are all a bunch of spineless cowards. I really don't know what is wrong with them. God I pray to leave this fucking compound because I don't want to be like them. Have you heard?

What?

Veronica, my sister, the one who prays a lot, has gotten a visa for Brazil. She's supposed to be going on a short vacation, but she's not coming back. I mean, who would want to come back to this shitty country? If anyone can escape with their head in place, I would advise that they leave immediately. Things aren't getting better and can only get worse.

So what is Veronica going to do in Brazil?

I don't know. She'll probably find some work.

Are you sure she won't be forced into prostitution?

I don't think so. That girl would probably commit suicide if anyone tried to force to do what she doesn't want to do.

Maybe you will join her in Brazil.

God, I wish I could play soccer.

Why?

It's another way to escape from this country.

You know the guys who stay in apartment four are footballers.

Yes I suspected. There are always in track suits.

Yes and they are always going for training, morning and evening. But I tell you, that's also a very hard road to travel. Those guys see hell but the payback is very good. The local league is useless. The coaches and referees are corrupt and are always looking for bribes. As a player, your talent counts for nothing if you don't have the right connections or are unable to buy your way into the big time.

Is that so?

Bro, it is a jungle out there. If you stay trying to make it in the local league, you'll only get old trying. The mafias control everything. The footballers belong to the mafia. The coaches and referees are at the center of the mafia. They make the rules and they break them. They tell you you're good when you're shit and leave the good ones out in the cold until they grow old with disappointment. Talent counts for shit in the local league bro. You just snoop around and try finding out for yourself. It's better to break into the international scene. That's where it's all happening and that's where the bucks are to be made. All the players and officials that make any headway in the local league are believers in voodoo. They practice voodoo and if you do not join them, they let you know you don't belong and ask you to leave. My mother would kill me if she even suspects I am thinking of joining a voodoo cult, but you need a foothold in the local league so that when foreign scouts come calling you have a forum to display you talents. If they find you on the field here, then arrangements can be made for you to go abroad and have a proper trial. A visa and everything would be arranged for you and then all you have to do is prepare yourself for war when you get over there. You can then be prepared to break everything, your head, your arms and your legs. You know you are in good hands then. You know nothing can happen to you if you get hurt because the people in charge value and respect talent. But here talent counts for shit. Here you're on your own if you can't do the voodoo dance and drink toad's blood. Bro, it isn't easy I tell you. You break a leg and you're gone even if you have a proper contract. A contract here isn't worth the paper it is on. You might as well wipe you arse with it.

So are you going to try your luck with soccer?

I might, but what I want to be is a rude boy.

What do you mean?

I'm prepared to do anything to survive. This country is fucked. The criminals are in charge and so the rules of the game have changed. If you sit there thinking that the good shall inherit the earth then you're totally fucked. You have to be as mean as the meanest of them, if not meaner, to survive. I'm prepared to go to Sierra Leone, Angola, or the Congo. I am prepared to go to Casablanca to try my luck. I want to trade in oil and precious minerals. This is what tough men do. I am tired to sleeping with pussies waiting for cheap hand-outs. It's not worth it. The insults are just not worth it. I'd rather die of hunger and thirst in the desert than continue to live with my family and not be able to help out. I have to be the man. I have to be able to put good food on the table. I don't give a fuck what anybody thinks, I will be a rude boy. I have seen the light. All these games of hide-and-seek the government is playing with our lives no longer deceive me.

I'm going to get out and get mine. I'm ready to go to the forests lying beyond the ancient city of Ibadan, Luanda, Maputo, or Harare in search of stuff such as tin concentrates, cola, genies, bush babies, timber, magnesium, zinc concentrates, gem diamonds, copper ore, colbalt, uranium, tungsten ore, industrial diamonds, silver, gold, crude oil, tantalum, or niobium. Anything that would bring money falls within my sphere of interest. I am ready to buy and sell anything.

But you don't have any start-off capital.

Well that's why I decided to be a rude boy.

How exactly are you going to make it as a rude boy?

Well I'm going to go to the south where the oil is. My mum comes from there. Things are happening there. The youths are restless. They're taking what's theirs. All these foreign companies have been ripping us off for so long. I'm going to get me an AK 47 and parade the swamps looking for those foreign blood-suckers. They have to start paying taxes for looting our wealth and all the environmental pollution they are causing. I've had enough of all this shit. How can you be so rich and so poor at the same time? It's not natural. Go to the south and see how everything has been ruined. Rivers dark with oil. Fishes belly up. Farmlands destroyed. People are starving. No roads, no hospitals, no schools. So what future do the youths have? None at all and that's why they take up arms. They have nothing to lose. When you have nothing to lose you fight like a motherfucker.

Do you believe you can fight?

Why not? What have I got to lose? I have no job and I have no hope of getting one. My sisters think I'm nothing. My mother won't get off my case and for what? What I have done? Is it because I don't have a job? Is it my fault that the national economy is fucked up? Was I part of the bunch of scoundrels that emptied the treasury? Did I get a penny from the looting? I mean this is simply unfair. I've never had any shit in my arse. It's now or never.

So what has your personal condition to do with the problems of the youths in the country?

Everything bro. If things were ok, then I wouldn't be here scratching my balls from morning to night with nothing to do and no one giving a shit. My family can't help me. My father has forgotten about us. In fact, he doesn't want to see us. I don't know what we did to him. I just want to show him that I'm not a failure. I want to help my mother even though she gives me a lot of shit. I want to move my family out of this dirty, stinking yard. There's no privacy, no security, no nothing. I'm sick and tired of this sort of life. It is better to die than continue to tolerate this kind of shit. Now is the time to act. Even if I die being a rude boy, at least I'll know I tried. I'll know that I did my best. Here, it's the same old shit everyday. You've got to take your future in your own hands. You got to go out there and hustle. Look at my sisters. They go out each and every day to work. I have to contribute my quota of hustle to the family. I can't let my father and his whore of a wife have the last laugh. I've got to show that I can do something, run some serious shit on the streets. Look at my mates that we went to school with. Mark is a big drug lord in Malaga. Louis hangs out in Rio de Janeiro with the big boys sipping cognac and champagne. He fucks the most beautiful models on the on the beaches of Rio. His mum told me he called the other day. I was smarter at school than those guys. They were looking up to me. I used to beat the shit out of them. Now look where I am and look where they are. No comparison at all. I can't even be hired to shine their shoes. It's now or never to roll the dice.

So to roll the dice, you will be a rude boy.

Yup. That's deal. I've got to make it happen.

Good luck to you Chidi.

Thanks bro. I need it.

It was time for Chidi to start making rounds of Internet cafés in the neighborhood. Con artists needed him to draft fake business letters and proposals on account of his proficiency in English. He made some loose change doing that sort of thing. He took pictures of naked girls, which he put on the Internet to lure men. The deal was that the girls would pretend to be in love with their matches, but they needed money to pay their school fees. Or they needed money for pay the hospital bills of their sick, indigent mothers. Or they needed to buy tickets to come and see their Internet lovers. But the male con artists were the most aggressive. They were always drafting all kinds of business proposals about oil deals, money to be claimed at the bank account of some rich deceased person, wanting advice on investment options in offshore regions, updating Internet banking services, and all manner of financial transactions. Chidi was paid cigarette money for his services. But if they struck success with a scam, then he would be paid more. It took a lot of effort and even more luck to strike gold.

Scam artists who do well in this line of business invested a great deal on achieving success. Errand boys were sent all over the coast of West Africa to dispatch letters by snail mail to countries in the northern hemisphere. Expensive hotels had to be booked for unsuspecting victims of a scam. Bogus apartments had to be rented and disguised as offices. Business suits had to be purchased for those taking part in the scam. Potential victims had to be impressed in every way. There were expensive lunches with top-level government functionaries to be bought. There were all-night parties at exclusive clubs with girls that had to be paid. A proper chair of a scam network worth his salt must do his homework and preparations thoroughly. The preparations involved both the actual physical level and the metaphysical dimension. The physical level didn't pose many challenges apart from finances. A scam network had to get itself ready by providing the required infrastructure; offices, fax machines, computers, Xerox machines, dubious attorneys and policemen, hotel rooms, chauffeurs, bodyguards, hired assassins, high-class hookers and so on. Only the big boys could provide this range of necessities.

The metaphysical level was the difficult part. The ogre of lucre asks you,

All right, you want some serious dough, can you give what I need in return?

And then you ask,

What do you need?

It laughs. You are nonplussed and demand to know.

I want the blood and the soul of your mother, it says. Or I want the blood of all your unborn children. Or you shall accommodate a cobra in your office for the rest of your days and if the cobra dies, you shall die as well. Or I want the blood of your wife, I know you love her but that's what I want.

Many men back off at this stage and are stricken by madness so as not to reveal what they had seen or heard. They are not permitted to see the ogre and live to refuse his demands. Instead, they shall lose their minds and then die. Those who have the guts and livers to provide the ogre with its demands invariably strike gold, but at a great price. They will lose their mothers, who stood by them when the world had cast them out. They will lose the one and only love of their lives. They will spend their days accommodating a cobra whose existence spells death for many loved ones. They will have to endure the curse of infertility. For men with hearts of steel, these conditions are bearable as long they are accompanied by an unrestricted flow of cash. In order for cash to set them free, they shall consume the blood of their mothers, their wives, and their children, and then the intractable spirit of money shall fuck with them until they can no longer stand its pussy.

They shall spend and consume until they become sick at the sight of money. Money will follow them into the bathroom when they want to have a bath. Money will follow when they go to the toilet to take a shit. Money will spread its legs for them when they can no longer get a hard-on. Money shall be their cologne that reeks throughout the town. Money will follow them everywhere they go and cause an ugly scene when they are dying for some peace and silence. Money will wrap their brains around its finger and do their thinking for them. Money will chase all their true friends away and fill their houses with sycophants, hopeless junkies, thieves, liars, dickheads who lick their shit and say what arseholes they are when behind their backs; relatives they never knew, relatives who once derided them and plotted countless times to kill them, hookers who turn them into incurable alcoholics, cunts who hurl them into an endless well of dissatisfaction.

Money will become the relentless mosquito that makes an unstoppable buzzing in your ears. Money is the shark that never sleeps and talks to you all day long. Money is the companion who tells you it can't go away when you need to sleep. Money picks you up and takes you for a late night dance when you want to sleep. Money smells, money dances, money loves, money kills, money disowns, money dissolves, money evaporates, money torments, money irrepressible, money insurmountable, money relentless, money destroys.

Chidi was at a crossroads about what level he wanted to pursue his search for money. His con artist associates had been telling him it was time to take the plunge. Was his liver strong enough to endure the gore and ultimate self-destruction? Could he walk in the valley of death as corpses fell upon him? Could he keep smiling as he ate the flesh of his own mother in the ritual that abolished the division between the living and the dead? Would he vomit? Would he piss and shit his pants in fright? It was difficult to tell. He felt a little disappointed that he didn't know himself well enough. He couldn't say for sure where the limits of his fortitude lay. Life threatening situations are known to ignite unforeseen reserves of inner strength. That was what he was counting upon because he had no choice but to take the plunge. What did the current situation of his life amount to if not a form of death? So why not choose a more exciting form of existence that made the experience of death an organized blood feast?

Benjamin Pancho, who lived in an estate down the street, had found the courage to make the ultimate choice. He had been an anthropologist at a university, who was dissatisfied with his life. Like most people, he hated his job and hated his life. He talked with his cousin, Julius, who flew around with beings on the metaphysical level. Julius was a wealthy Internet fraudster and Benjamin Pancho wanted to be like him. He wanted money and power. First of all, Julius instructed Benjamin to find the excrement of a pregnant agama lizard, which he had to place on a rock amid two dry twigs. The rock must be located in a wasteland filled with garbage. The excrement and twigs must receive the warmth of the mid-day sun for at least four hours. When this was done, the denizens of the netherworld would be ready to receive him.

Benjamin did as he was told. Weeks later, he was invited to the formal initiation ritual. He was blinded-folded and led by the voices of the half-dead into the arch chamber of the dead. He wore nothing except a brown and green wrap around his waist. He was told to kneel to receive instructions from the custodians of the shrine.

We are here tonight to receive a new initiate. We are not here for games. This is not something for boys or the faint-hearted. We are here to dine with the gods. You have to have a hard belly. You have to renounce your connection with the values and expectations of the living and receive the blessings of those who stand at the gates of the kingdom of the dead. Here, life and the death do not intermingle. There is no sitting on the fence. If you do, you would be brought down by madness and death. Those in the so-called world of the living are blind and do not see. They are worthless because they are just floating about aimlessly. Therefore, they are expendable. Once you enter into the kingdom of the dead, you shall know the extent of the unworthiness of the living. Your father is useless. Your mother is useless. Your brothers and sisters are useless. Your children are useless. Except for their souls, flesh, and blood for rituals to abolish suffering. We need bones from your blood line to make your wish come true. If you want to subdue the spirit of money, then you must be able to give what you most value in return. Are you prepared to give something in order to depart from the world of sufferers?

Yes my lord.

What are you prepared to give?

My children.

Is that all?

My wife.

Good. Very good.

You have made a pact with the kingdom of the dead. This pact has been sealed with the blood of your wife and children. It is a pact that cannot be broken. You shall defile the sanctity of your wife and have sex with your children. These are mere earthly distractions, but in metaphysical terms, they amount to clearing the way for the entry of untold riches for you. Welcome my friend to the kingdom of the dead where all the decisions concerning the galaxies are made.

Here, you find the womb of power, the sole power from which everything flows. Here, dark and white waters meet in a marriage that takes place on the face of the moon and when they have offspring they are angels who are in fact serpents. Welcome my friend.

Thank you my Lord.

After his initiation, Benjamin Pancho came into sudden and unexplained wealth. He bought a mansion at one end of Enitan's streets and spent money turning it into a landmark. Every week, he bought a new luxurious car which was imported. Parties were thrown each time to celebrate the purchases. All the girls in town wanted to his girlfriend. Each week, cows were slaughtered. Beggars who sat at the corners of the street grew fat on Benjamin's generosity. The stray dogs became lazy and pacific on account of the endless feasts. When Benjamin came and went, he was accompanied a fleet of expensive cars. Hangers-on jostled for his attention. Relatives quarreled over who would wash and iron his clothes. Friends betrayed one another in order to please him. Intelligent men made fools of themselves in order to be admitted into his inner sanctum. When drunk with joy, Benjamin and his gathering of arse lickers shot holes into the walls of his mansion. The next day, workmen were hired to repair the damage. And then holes were shot into the walls again. The workmen made a small fortune plastering holes made by gunshots. They even advised Benjamin about what guns to buy in order to get the best holes.

One evening, after the usual bout of revelry, Benjamin brought out his cock and said it was tired. Asked why, he said his cock had entered every available pussy in town and there were no more fresh holes left. He was tired of sticking his toes into women's fannies because he could no longer fuck. He was tired of being entertained by naked girls who fought viciously in his swimming pool just to catch his eye while he puffed cigars and smoked joints of marijuana. He wanted to retire his cock. In other words, he wanted to get married.

Word went around town that Benjamin was looking for a wife. Suddenly, shy girls became unabashed exhibitionists. Women who had no where to go dressed up and paraded the length and breadth of the street hoping to catch Benjamin's attention. Widows and middle-aged women threw their shawls and head gear on the ground for him to walk over. Street musicians came over every night with their assortment of talking drums to sing his praises. When the eulogies became too overwhelming, Benjamin fired shots into the air at three o'clock in the morning.

Benjamin Pancho's hangers-on went about putting their sisters and female cousins on notice. A big shot needed a wife, and if they played their cards right, there was a ticket out of penury available. Benjamin's henchmen started to bring women to the mansion with the hope that he would find one to his liking. Benjamin eventually indicated interest in Jennifer Funtan, a stunning beauty who had been brought by Papa Frankie the Ball Head. Papa Frankie was one of the boys who made everyone laugh. Jennifer Funtan was a distant relative and he wanted to use her in strengthening his relationship with Benjamin Pancho.

Benjamin was besotted as soon as he set eyes on Jennifer. She was a dark beauty with almond eyes and even more beautiful legs. Almost six feet tall, she had the most exquisite manners. Benjamin bought a scarlet sports car because he thought it would reveal better the glow of her complexion and accentuate the length of her gorgeous legs. When they went cruising, he opened the sun roof so that her hair could flow behind her like a dark stream trailing her tilted head. On such occasions, she wore designer sunshades and crossed her legs. He had finally found someone to complement him in a way that concealed his numerous deficiencies—Jennifer Funtan over and over. It's your day girl, go for it. Jennifer knew she had a great sense of style, but she hadn't realized the precise extent of its effect on people. That wasn't her business. Her business was to look good and be good.

In a few weeks, Benjamin Pancho was talking about marriage. Jennifer Funtan wanted to finish the biochemistry course she was reading. Benjamin objected that a program in biochemistry shouldn't delay their future. He simply couldn't wait to make her his wife. She shrugged and told him to go ahead.

The stag party that was arranged at the mansion was the talk of the decade. Liquor was flown in from overseas. Guys hung about in air-conditioned lounges downing Hennessy as if it were water. Chicks from various universities looking like models were brought into the mansion by the truckload. Coke was served in glistening bowls of silver. Crate upon crate of chilled champagne was supplied. This is the life! Brothers and gangsters kept saying as techno-beats seeped into the bones. After this, there is no other life, said the brothers and gangsters as they cocked their heads in the shadows to spy panties underneath the micro minis. This is the life, said the brothers and gangsters as they tried to decide what was making them dizzy—the coke, the brandy, or simply the winterlike chill of air-conditioners. This is the life, and may it not end. Death to the bugger who even dares to think otherwise. The party went on for three long days.

A policeman who had been hired to provide security got fairly drunk and was pissing on the front lawn of the

71

mansion. Benjamin's attention was drawn to the man who told him to piss off.

What's your problem?

What's my problem?

You're the one whose got a problem. You're an exploiter, a bloodsucker. In fact you are shit.

What did I do to you?

What didn't you do to me?

No, seriously tell me.

For three days, I have been looking after you and your guests. And have you once asked me if I was ok?

But I instructed a girl to provide you with anything you need, food and drink.

Food and drink. Is that all a man needs? Do I look glutton to you? It is said in the Bible, man must not live by bread alone.

So what do you want now?

Now he asks.

Please tell me.

Do you think I'm made of wood? Can you just arrange for one of those girls in there for me, to protect me from the cold?

You have to talk to them yourself.

What are you saying, can't you order one of them to take care of me?

Look I have no time for this rubbish. Get a girl yourself.

I won't forget this. You are exploiting me.

I have paid you more than you receive in a year.

Fuck off! You're an exploiter. I'll let my colleagues at the barrack know that! They shouldn't take any job from you. You use people.

Benjamin Pancho saw that it was useless talking to the cop and returned inside to be with his guests and hangers-on. He had had a successful stag party and that was all that mattered. The wedding proper took place four months later. There was a traditional marriage at his hometown, Obondizo. Fleets of cars left the city for Obondizo two days before the traditional ceremony. All went well except that a couple of drunks fell off rooftops when trying to pee. The white wedding also went well.

After months of haggling with Jennifer's family, she was finally his. She slept in his bed and sometimes prepared his meals. He didn't want her to have to do anything. He just wanted her lying in bed all day and day-dreaming about the children she would bear him. He didn't want her bothering her pretty little head about what to wear, what car to drive, or what drink to have. She had a coterie of domestics at her disposal. She had chauffeurs assigned to her.

But Jennifer liked to do things for herself. She had been used to looking after herself since he father passed away when she was nine. She found it boring to lie in bed daydreaming as her husband wanted. She wanted to build a life of her own and not become part of Benjamin's daily furniture. Apart from his money, there was nothing about him that she found of interest. They had different ideas about shopping, interior design, manners, friendship, leisure, and entertainment. But she had also been trained to yield to her husband. She had been taught about the importance of avoiding conflict and maintaining domestic tranquility. So she withdrew into herself and floated through everything. It was as if she closed her eyes to what she didn't like. She learned to tolerate almost everything.

One evening, when Jennifer was returning home after a day out with friends, she noticed she was being followed by a black truck. In fear, she thought she was being trailed by a gang of armed robbers, so she stepped on the accelerator. The truck followed, matching her speed. Jennifer swerved into her neighborhood and screeched to a stop by the locked gates of the mansion. The truck in pursuit opened fire on her car. She died instantly. It turned out that the men in the truck were cops who had had a hunch that the car was stolen. Jennifer's body was riddled with bullets. It was as if the men who fired at her had an aversion to natural beauty. Her scalp was torn apart and blood flowed through her lush hair. Her intestines spilled from her belly and lay smattered around the seat and the floor of the car. There was blood everywhere. Blood on the windshield, blood on the door windows. Her formerly white outfit was no longer recognizable. The car looked as if it belonged to the president of a banana republic and had been involved in a coup d'etat. The intention, all occupants must perish beyond recognition.

Benjamin Pancho was distraught. It seemed he no longer had anything to live for. Just when he had found true happiness for once in his life, it disappeared from view like the unpleasant deception of a mirage. He started to believe that he was cursed. He then traced the beginning of woes to the time when he got initiated into the cult of the dead. The influx of material riches into his life had been predicated on the blood of his wife and his children. But in his wife, he had found the love he had never had, the love that had granted him happiness. Now that he had more money than three generations could spend, it was time to devote himself to securing his happiness. It occurred to him that he could never find true happiness until the covenant he had with the cult of the dead was broken, until he returned in spirit to the world of the living. He sank into depression as images of Jennifer continued to flit through his mind and haunt him. He believed that he was responsible for her death. Jennifer Funtan was gone and he would be haunted as long as he lived by the memory of her incomparable beauty. He had mortgaged the blood of his wife for material wealth without thinking of the possible consequences. He wanted to be free of the cult of the dead; but he also knew that could only come with an astronomical price.

Benjamin Pancho chased away all his hangers-on and henchmen. Seeing them around only triggered painful memories. He was determined that his life take a new turn. He spent nights and days mulling over what to do and how to go about it. If he broke the covenant with the cult of the dead, he would either go insane or die. Worse still, he might endure both madness and sudden death within a brief space of time. He had been warned explicitly of the repercussions of breaking the conditions of the covenant. But he kept beating himself up for a way out. He kept thinking that there must be a solution to his abject spiritual imprisonment and impoverishment.

Then it struck Benjamin to approach the white garment church down his street for spiritual redemption. He would confess that he had joined the cult of the dead and confide that he wanted to break away from it and rejoin the world of the living. In order to emphasize the seriousness of his plight, he bought a gift of ten live cows and seven dozen white chickens and presented it to the church. The church's elders received the gift with immense gratitude. Benjamin told them he would return in seven days to make a request. The elders replied, saying all children of the world were always welcome into the church.

After seven days, Benjamin Pancho told the leaders of the church his ordeal. They listened with rapt attention and conferred among themselves for a few minutes while he waited outside the office. After a few minutes, they called him back in and told him that he would be able to re-enter the world of the living if they performed some religious rituals at his mansion. Benjamin Pancho was delighted. He felt he had some hope in overcoming his crisis.

Hallelujah! Hallelujah! Hallelujah! Hallelujah! Hallelujah! Hallelujah! Hallelujah!

Go, and be well our son; we shall see you again soon.

A few days later, twelve elders of the church visited Benjamin at his mansion. None of them wore shoes. Most of them had long disheveled hair. Their robes were sparkling white and all of them had red or blue sashes around their waists. They knelt on the front lawn and prayed. With them were little brass and silver cisterns bearing incense, red candles, bottles of olive oil, bottles of blessed water, paintings of Christ, paintings of the twelve apostles, and paintings of gardens and bowls of fruit. They arranged the items carefully around the lawn. The church elders began a seven-day dry fast. Benjamin was instructed also to fast from six in the morning to six in the evening for seven days. The cleansing process had begun. The elders spoke in tongues and cursed the cult of the dead admonishing it to let Benjamin go. They denied that power resided with the cult as it claimed, and countered that they were the custodians of power over wealth, which they held by proxy but were free to use as they saw fit. For seven days and nights, they went around the mansion casting out evil spells. They walked throughout the rooms of the mansion chastising evil spirits. Spirals of incense unfurled before them and rose in their wake. They spoke in different languages. They spoke in Hebrew and Amharic. They sang religious songs of victory and redemption. Benjamin Pancho clapped his hands and followed their lead, praying that he be set free.

After seven days, the ritual of cleansing was over. The elders gave Benjamin conditions to ensure the continued success of the ritual. He had to break away completely from the cult. He had to dissociate himself from his former associates, hangers-on, and henchmen. He had to renounce the life of a party freak and commit himself to the path of virtue and modesty. Not the least bit of flamboyance could be left in his manner. He had to be modest in thought, appearance, and deed. He had to give away a substantial part of his wealth to the church and other charitable organizations. He had to walk in the path of light for the rest of his life. He had to renounce the way of darkness. He was told that if he kept any sponges, nails, shells, stones, or mortars in his belly, he ought to say, so they could be expelled. He was told to name all the witches he patronized so that the bonds between them could be broken. He was told to produce the charms he was given by the cult. He wasn't to keep any occultic mementoes of his past life because every chain of continuity must be broken. He was exhorted to pray and think of every material link to his old life so it could be sought out and broken. He must break the spell of continuity that held him in bondage.

Benjamin prayed and grew agitated about occultic links to his past. He produced every item he could remember from his past; the elders burned them all on the front lawn of his mansion. Talismans, miniature mortars and pestles, tortoise shells, shrine brooms, figurines, rusty nails, parrots' feathers, crocodile oil, caked herbal concoctions in little bottles, mud sculptures, masks from the Congo, ritual attire, loads and loads of stuff were thrown onto a bonfire. More prayers and days of fasting followed, followed in turn by days of rejoicing and victory feasts. Eventually, Benjamin Pancho was informed the bond between him and the cult of the dead had been broken. He was now free to lead a new life.

Months passed and Benjamin maintained his vow to break with his former associates. Many of them tried to reach him in his known houses and hang-outs, but were disappointed. He had perfected a series of disguises that made him especially difficult to recognize. He sold all his luxurious vehicles and bought a couple of run-down secondhand cars, but mostly he preferred to go around in hired taxicabs. He slept in obscure hotels, which he changed every few days. He went around looking like an out-of-work laborer. Anyone from his former life who had seen him in his new get-up would think he was having a nervous breakdown. No one was even sure about which country was his new base. There were rumors about him living in Liberia, Sierra Leone, Austria, Belgium, Mexico. No one was sure. There were periodic reports of sightings of figures resembling Benjamin, and all this passed into local lore and got embellished in different ways. There were rumors that he was planning a huge comeback. His former hangers-on were usually the main sources of these rumors. They boasted in seedy bars to curious onlookers about the fabulous extent of Benjamin Pancho's wealth.

Gossips claimed brandy and whiskey flowed out of gold taps in Benjamin's mansion. They said they had lost most of their teeth from eating too much meat. There were stories of stray dogs and beggars getting sick from overeating. They recounted feasts that ran for weeks. Many butchers amassed fortunes due to Benjamin's patronage. His generosity was legendary. His girlfriends owned apartments in Paris, Milan, and Los Angeles. He gave cars to his henchmen on their birthdays. He offered them businesses for winning drinking contests. He gave hotels to those who had the most impressive sexual prowess. There were rumors that Benjamin was not a real human being because of his extraordinary larger-than-life quality. He was some celestial spirit with special powers.

There was no end to the rumors. Benjamin Pancho was the ultimate monarch of the future. He was not a spirit for the present times. His visionary sensibility had granted him vistas no ordinary human being could grasp. Benjamin

Pancho was way ahead of everyone else. Benjamin Pancho could not die. He was painstakingly planning his return and resurrection. He was too good to die. He was a spirit and so could not die. They ought to prepare themselves for his return and make his final ascent as smooth as possible. They speculated about his mode of transport upon his return. Some said he would come in the biggest airplane. Some said he would land in a helicopter. Some said he would sneak into the neighborhood in the middle of the night and throw the most lavish party ever. Some said his entry would be announced by an advance party of the world's most beautiful models. Some said he would abolish hunger and poverty. Some said he was planning to be the president of the country. The rumors multiplied about Benjamin Pancho's whereabouts and date of return. He had passed into the realm of myth.

In reality, Benjamin Pancho continued to keep a low profile. He took to wearing different types of hats to disguise himself. He hardly left his mansion and stayed indoors praying and fasting. The elders of the church decided that he needed someone, a new wife, to add some spice to his otherwise drab existence. They introduced him to Mercy Majuku. She was said to possess all the credentials to make a good wife. She modest, pious, and amiable. She was also said to come from a good background. Benjamin and Mercy dated for a couple of months and then married quietly in the white garment church. There were no guests from Benjamin's side. But Mercy's five sisters all attended the church ceremony together with their mother.

Benjamin noticed that a couple of Mercy's sisters were more beautiful than she. He hated himself for making such a distasteful mental note. The newlyweds slipped quietly in domestic life with Mercy dutifully trying to live up to the customary expectations of a wife. Benjamin retained a few domestics to assist in running the mansion. Three of Mercy's sisters moved in with her to keep her company. The household seemed decent and well-organized. They all prayed together at morning and before going to bed at night. Benjamin usually led the prayers. He had become a skilled leader of prayers, evoking the good and declaiming the unseemly. He paused at the right moments to create suspense and emphasized important points at the appropriate interludes. His wife even encouraged him to become a deacon at the church.

The art of praying had long since become intertwined with performance and oratory. It was no longer simply an internal dialogue with the Almighty. It had become an advanced art of invocations, exhortations, declamations, and affirmations. It had become a continual act of affirmation in the face of defeat and victimhood. Passages of denunciation were followed by fervent affirmations of victory. Negativity and positivity were juxtaposed not only to reveal the immense distance between them but to cast into greater relief the sharp contrasts in their complexions. One needed the other to acquire specificity and character. The best preachers knew how to exploit this relation of contrasts; they knew how to connect it to the mystery and menace inherent in human existence. This seemingly basic foundation opened up to an infinite expanse of spiritual and existential possibilities. It contained the complex history of humankind in a stark dichotomy of apparent simplicity. In a parallel universe, the blues, as a form of uplifting and therapeutic music, is both simple and complex. It begans with the trauma of coping with plantation life. But out of this somewhat deceptive art form, a diverse series of performance arts had emerged that, in the ostensible distance from the originary form, display no easily noticeable traces. But upon closer examination, the traces mark and influence each and every undercurrent of creative expression that can be found. Accordingly, the founding contrasts between good and evil in the act of prayer are an equation for the complex history of the world reduced to manageable simplicity. They are an index of a continual contestation between the forces of complexity and the inclinations toward simplicity.

Days filled with prayers and fasting went by. Mercy was happy with her husband and she soon became pregnant. She felt very fortunate to be carrying the child of such a considerate man. They hugged and kissed in the full view of their household. Mercy didn't mind even though she could be quite shy at times. She was determined to make her home a haven of peace and decency. She was prepared to bring children into the world who would honor her husband's name. True, she had heard rumors that he wasn't a man, but a supernatural being who had donated his soul to denizens of the land of the spirits. She had been warned that she and her children would perish if she agreed to make Benjamin her husband. People claimed he had slept with more than twelve thousand women and had used their souls to make money. They said his money was not of this world and that it probably emerged from some netherworld. They claimed no woman could live with him because he had no conscience and absolutely no understanding of the concept of humanity. Women who survived affairs with him complained of being excavated by some mysterious force. They said they were not the same after sharing his bed. But Mercy was no longer bothered about Benjamin's doubtful past now that she could see that he was a completely changed man.

Still, the rumors continued. Some claimed that Benjamin until made love in cemeteries at odd hours, preferably at the stroke of midnight; he wasn't a happy man. They claimed he wore black robes while performing his rituals of deviant sex. They said black cats swirled and shrieked when he reached orgasm. They claimed the shrieks of the black cats had been the beginning of their misery. Some claimed that he engaged in cemetery sex when he needed raw cash. They said he released clouds of confetti after each performance of cemetery sex. They said that after having sex, he wiped off vaginal fluids with a piece cut from his black robes. Some of the women said that when they stood up from a grave stone, a sudden gust of wind almost knocked them down. They said that he kept most of the semen on the piece he cut from his robes. They claimed that after such deviant sex, his already incredible wealth had multiplied a thousandfold. They claimed human blood was the primary source of his wealth. They said he was irresistible once he set his eyes upon you. They said it is impossible to refuse him an invitation to visit a cemetery after midnight. They said that at such moments, the glow of his eyes had become unreal, supernatural. They claimed women followed him down to the cemetery as if in a trance. They said it is absolutely impossible to resist the force of his will.

Mercy's husband had been portrayed as a creature of an unnatural order, a wrecker of traditional mores, a nihilist who had come to replace stability with outright upheaval. Even worse, it was said that he annihilated all those who stood in way. He was thus to be avoided at all cost. The only interesting thing about him was his wealth. If it were possible to enjoy some of his largesse, then it should be done. But it usually came with a heavy price. Nonetheless, she tried to forget about all the tales of despicable decadence, bestiality, and deviance about her husband that filled her ears.

Mercy nee Majuku was convinced that whatever was her husband's past stayed in the past. He was now a changed man as confirmed by his newly-acquired status as a prayer warrior and as an active participant in the white garment church down the street. These were quite impressive credentials that would sway any believer in the possibilities for radical transformation of the human spirit. She believed in her man and the future of the baby they were going to have together. She believed hearts can be changed and that horrible nightmares can be dispelled through the power of prayer. She was determined to make her marriage work and intended to build a family with her husband.

But Benjamin had started to feel restless. He felt hemmed in by the constrictions of the white garment church that had offered him a new life. He was getting bored with the preoccupations of the elders of the church. All they ever seemed to be concerned about was the donation of tithes, the necessity of generous alms-giving to make improvements on the church building, and the organization of harvests to broaden their social cachet. They were always inviting him to chair such events because he made generous donations. It wasn't mainly the pressure to make donations that really bothered him. It the compulsion of having to enter into social networks that he would rather avoid that troubled him.

Mercy, on the other hand, was usually at ease on such occasions, as there was an understated quality in her personality. She managed to deflect undue scrutiny while eliciting trust and confidence in her associates. Benjamin would sometimes send her to represent him while he remained in the mansion. But he was beginning to feel trapped within the fresh rhythms of life. All he did was sit at home and play the househusband. He was only in his mid-thirties and so he still had a tremendous amount of energy to burn. Mercy was a good wife, but he wanted more out of life. Neither had he estimated the great difference between the frenetic pace of his life as a former international fraudster and the slow burn of his existence as an adherent of a white garment denomination. The disparity in lifestyles was slowly plunging him into an existential and psychological crisis. He needed some swing or he would go mad. He didn't always take into account the fact that only some months ago, he had been dangling between the scythe of death and the jagged jaws of insanity. His relative well-being was compelling him to ask more out of life.

Benjamin's thoughts began to stray toward Mercy's two sisters. The older one, Mandy, was twenty-three and blessed with a stunning figure. She didn't have as striking facial features as Mercy, due to a permanent redness of the eyes. She also had scars on her left temple from a car accident a couple of years back. But her figure compensated for all of that. She made Benjamin's blood boil with lust. He had taken to giving her huge smiles when he met her in the kitchen or when they found themselves alone in one of the lounges. She was a versatile cook who loved being in the kitchen, and Benjamin would always find occasion to fetch drinks and snacks when she was preparing a meal. One day, he couldn't resist the attraction caused by her tight-fitting jeans; he slapped her on the bum with a palm. Stunned, she looked over her shoulder to see Benjamin with a wide grin on his face.

I've got a lovely present for you.

Really? What is it?

It is the most expensive gift you've ever received.

Where is it?

Somewhere safe. But you must promise me first never to let anyone know I gave it to you. Not my wife, your mother, or your sisters. Not your friends; because if you, do the secret would be out.

What is it you want to give me?

I want to surprise you. Believe me, it's the best present anyone could ever give you in your life.

You're joking.

I'm not; I promise you.

When can I get it?

Tonight when I come to your bedroom. Remember to leave your door unlocked.

But why my bedroom?

Because as I told you, it is the most expensive gift you could ever receive in your life and I want it to be a secret between us. Please; I really mean it. Don't give me any problems. You're twenty-three or so, which means you ought to be mature about all this. You're not a little girl. If you behave yourself, I promise you there will be even more expensive presents for you. You won't ever have to suffer in your life. Tonight, at eleven o'clock, in your bedroom, your life will change completely. Please wait for me.

On that evening, Benjamin convinced his wife that he was too exhausted to watch any movies with her and that they ought to retire to bed. She agreed. she went into the bathroom for a bath. She took her time, taking care to use many of her jells and oils. She emerged naked and with a radiant glow. It was clear she wanted to have sex, but Benjamin pretended to be tired. He had other plans. Mercy slid beside him and splayed an arm over his body. She smelled enticing. She was whispering into his ear.

Baby, baby, baby.

She put a palm on his face and stroked his chin and temples gently. She was doing a good job of trying to get him aroused. She succeeded, but he had made other plans, which she must never know. She kept moaning baby, baby, baby until she fell asleep. Benjamin remained motionless for about ten minutes, and then, he gently removed her arm from his torso. He waited for a few more minutes to ensure she was truly asleep. She didn't budge, so he slid a leg off the bed onto the floor. He turned and looked at her face in the semi-darkness to see if her eyelids moved. They did not. He put his other foot on the floor and stood quietly. Tiptoing to his wardrobe, he fished out a diamond necklace from the side pocket of a coat he had purposely hung at the edge of the wardrobe within easy reach. He didn't bother to wear his slippers as he sneaked toward the door, which he opened with barely a squeak. He turned once more to regard Mercy's eyelids. They remained motionless. He squeezed through the partially open door and pulled it slightly closed behind him without completely shutting it. He had an alibi ready. If she asked him where he had gone, he would tell her he had gone to get some water.

He tiptoed down the passageway past a spare bathroom and a closet. He eventually came to Mandy's door. Turning the knob, he stealthily entered like a thief. Mandy's lights were on. Benjamin clutched the diamond necklace in his left palm.

Mandy, Mandy, I'm here.

Still groggy from sleeping, Mandy turned and tried to train her eyes on his blurry form. Although she had been expecting him before she felt asleep, she had drifted off thinking that he wasn't coming. Gradually, she remembered the rendezvous as Benjamin's form came into focus. Benjamin held up the piece of jewelry between a thump and finger toward the lamp above him to catch a glint of light.

What is that?

Guess.

I don't know. Please let me see.

Benjamin moved closer, holding out the necklace in front of him. Mandy sat up with the sheets falling away to reveal a pink t-shirt featuring Mickey Mouse. Benjamin wondered whether she was wearing any panties.

Please let me see.

On one condition.

What? Please let me see it.

You must also give me something in return.

What do you want?

You.

Benjamin moved closer to her bed and sat on the edge.

This is yours baby, you only have to cooperate.

Mandy lowered her head and stared down at the floor by her side. Benjamin had moved even closer to her and began caressing her thighs. He kissed her on the cheek while she kept her eyes fixed on the floor. He turned her face toward him sharply and kissed her on the mouth. She offered no resistance. He stroked her neck with the necklace so she could feel the texture of the diamonds as he kissed her. She tasted sweet. He stood suddenly and started to undress. Mandy picked up the necklace on the bed where he'd dropped it and examined the precious stones as they glimmered in the light. The glint made her fully awake.

Oh baby I've been waiting for this day for so long.

He moved to lie beside her. He had been nursing an erection ever since Mercy had tried to get him ready. Mandy barely noticed his erection as she was too preoccupied with studying her gift.

We've got to hurry before we alert somebody. Do you have any condoms?

Here's one.

Thank you my dear.

Mandy couldn't care less whether they were caught. It was his business if someone found out. She had done nothing wrong because he had come to her. She didn't go to him. All that concerned her was the present she had been given.

Benjamin pulled up her t-shirt and sucked Mandy's breasts greedily. Then he got her to lie back so he could kiss her breasts some more. Her large breasts became luminiscent with his spittle. Indeed, she wasn't wearing any panties and he couldn't bear the strain in his crotch any longer. He plunged into her and immediately descended into a murky, indescribable realm of pleasure and came quickly.

Benjamin hurriedly pulled up his shorts, adjusted his t-shirt, and tiptoed to the door. He pulled it open slowly and peered to see if anyone was in the passage. Seeing no one, he sneaked out and walked hastily toward his bedroom. The door was still partially open as he had left it, meaning Mercy hadn't come out. He thought about going into the bathroom to wash off any lingering smell of sex but dropped the thought when he saw Mercy sleeping deeply. Gradually, he pulled both of his legs up into his matrimonial bed and heaved a sigh of relief. He felt vital once more. His life once again had the edge he was used to. He was once again a player who took high risks. He could feel the sharp impartiality of the knife's edge once more. He was Benjamin Pancho, the untamable wildebeest who uprooted shrubs and trees with the force of a tumultuous gale. He was Benjamin Pancho, who had previously eaten the bones of his detractors for breakfast. He was Benjamin Pancho, who had no fear of any man since he had the strength and ability to build empires. In his excitement about what had happened, he failed to sleep deeply.

In the morning when he went down into the kitchen, Mandy, assisted by Marilyn, was a making breakfast of eggs and bacon on toast with tea or coffee. Benjamin didn't always go for breakfast, and when he did, he preferred a plate of beans with pap. Marilyn, a stunning beauty in her own right, said good morning to him.

Mandy, aren't you going to say good morning to me?

Good morning.

How are you? Did you sleep well last night?

Yes. Thank you.

Great.

So what are you making for breakfast?

Egg, bacon, and toast.

Great. I love egg and toast.

How about you Marilyn, do you like egg bacon and toast?

I don't mind.

You don't seem to be too keen. Do you want me to take you guys out for dinner sometime?

That would be nice.

I'll speak with your elder sister and see what can be arranged.

Thank you sir.

Benjamin was satisfied that their little secret was intact. Mandy's composure indicated that she was not the kind to reveal such information. She was a big girl, he thought. Days went by. On the fifth day, Benjamin visited Mandy's bedroom again, this time carrying a gold wristwatch. He followed the pattern established on his first visit, waiting for Mercy to sleep and then tiptoing out of their bedroom, leaving the door ajar, so he could re-enter with minimum commotion. Again, he had pleasurable sex and had returned to his bed without arousing Mercy's attention. When church engagements called Mercy away, Benjamin would send Marilyn to the markets on errands so he could be alone with Mandy. On such occasions, they would have sex on the floor of the main lounge. It was lovely to lie on the rug and enjoy the chill of the powerful air-conditioner while they were at it.

Benjamin couldn't get enough of those moments. His secret life had provided him with a cracked mirror that reflected the facets of his being a monogamous situation had sought to stifle and deny him. His hidden existence had produced innumerable condiments on his otherwise drab dinner table. He only had to maintain his balance and keep his secret life distinct from his normal everyday existence. He didn't foresee any problems in enforcing these separate spheres of existence. Much as they must remain separate, he needed to be sustain them to endure the tedium of marriage.

Up to then, Benjamin hadn't even really given much thought to why he had married. It occurred to him that he had yielded to wishes of the elders of the church. It also struck him that he had been trying to fill the void left in the wake of Jennifer Funtan's passing. Jennifer's demise was the final straw that had plunged him into the prison of his current marriage. He would have run mad if he had remained alone. In this respect, the elders of the church had been accurate. He needed another life to substitute for his former existence. He needed a burden that would exceed or at least equal his old agony. He needed a void that would replace the old void. That was what survival was about. The endless substitution of vacuums with voids. The ceaseless production of interruptions within a given space to displace silence and decay.

Benjamin had been mistaken in thinking that the severance of his covenant with the cult of the dead would lead to a state of permanent contentment. He had been wrong in thinking that he would have the perseverance to bask within a margin of shadows for the rest of his life. He had displayed a lack of foresight in deeming it possible to continue breathing in drab and worn clothing, twiddling his thumbs and perpetually recoiling from the light. These were the conditions to achieve safety and personal well-being. But now that his well-being seemed assured, he needed to break out of his cold confinement and feel the heat of the stars. He sorely needed the taste of hot spice in his mouth to be able stomach the agony of enduring yet another day.

His dilemma was both simple and complex. He wanted to walk on a tightrope like a dare devil, risking death. This compulsion constituted a vital part of his make up. At the same time, he wanted to stay alive and maintain an impenetrable façade of normalcy. For him, Mercy represented the façade of normalcy. She was the open, safe, simplicity by day. Mandy was the secret spice filched by night. She represented the opposite polarity of complexity, the font of possibility and transgression.

Benjamin was surprised that he had found two vital complementary individuals for his life in a single family. But what brought much-needed balance and fulfillment also carried the stigma of taboo. Fuck stigma he thought. He would run with the winds in the dark and hope he didn't run into trees, as the thrill of the risk made him feel more alive. His affiliation with the cult of the dead had abolished the distinct dichotomy between simplicity and complexity. In their world, life and death lose their singularity. The unknown becomes doubly unknowable and infinitely more ominous. Added layers of complexity are brought into the equation and simplicity is finally discarded. This is a severe truncation, an ongoing abortion that has no end. These were the features that Benjamin Pancho did not anticipate or understand; he was not prepared to deal with them. That was why it was necessary for him to break his covenant with the cult of the dead and return to the inexhaustible mysteries of the living.

For several weeks, Benjamin continued to have sex with Mandy, either in her bedroom at night or during the day when Mercy was away. Mercy was now heavily pregnant and had started to prepare for the arrival of the baby. Lately, she had been feeling slightly uneasy, but couldn't put her finger on the reason. One night, unable to sleep, she noticed her husband was fidgeting; she felt him sneaking out of bed. She waited until he had slipped through the door and then tiptoed after him to see where he was going. She observed him going down left through the passageway instead of going the opposite direction where the staircase was located. She ducked back into the bedroom just as he was starting to turn for a final look around before he disappeared into Mandy's bedroom. Mercy was distraught but still had the presence of mind to go down the passageway slowly. She didn't open the door immediately, but waited until she knew things had settled. When she opened the door, which had been left unlocked, she saw Benjamin naked atop Mandy.

Mandy!

She screamed,

You bitch!

Benjamin leapt from Mandy and started to struggle into his shorts. His eyes were wide from surprise, fear, and perplexity. His entire frame tensed with uncustomary tension. Mandy merely used the sheets to cover her breasts and made no attempt to leave the bed.

Mercy, please, I can explain. It is the work of bad spiritual forces.

Mandy, how dare you after all I've done for you! You bitch. You husband snatcher.

Mandy pouted but remained silent. Mercy lurched at her and struck her on the face. By then, Benjamin had managed to get into his shorts and flung himself on Mercy, trying to restrain her. She bit him on the arm and tried to strike Mandy again. Mandy jumped off the bed yelling to be left alone as she reached for a bed sheet to cover her naked body. The smugness had had disappeared from her face and was replaced by a combination of fear and confusion. She didn't know what to do and just wanted to get out of Mercy's way.

This bitch is leaving this house this night.

Please calm down Mercy.

No! She must leave this house tonight.

But it's impossible. Where would she go?

I don't care. She can go to hell for all I care.

Please Mercy, let us settle this thing amicably. This is all work of the devil.

Shut up. So you didn't know it was the devil's work when you were fucking her.

Please don't talk like that, it is unChristian.

So you didn't know that what you were doing was unChristian? Look, if you want peace in this house, either she goes or we break up.

Please let's all go to sleep and settle this thing tomorrow.

No! We have to settle everything now. You can still talk. You're a shameless man. You're not even a real man. No real man would sleep with his wife's sister. But I will deal with you in my own time.

Please Mercy, let's go to sleep for now. Let's not wake up the neighbors. I beg you. I beg you! Please Mercy let's go to bed.

In fact, this bitch is not sleeping in this room today. Go downstairs and sleep in the lounge. And leave this house first thing tomorrow morning. I can never forgive you for what you've done.

Please Mercy, it's enough. Let's go to our room.

I will still deal with you later Benjamin Pancho, or whatever you call yourself. You are a totally useless and shameless man. I'll make sure you regret this day as long as you live. You! I said to go downstairs and sleep in lounge! I don't want your useless spirit on the same floor as me.

Mandy had tears running down her face as she went out of the room with a bed sheet around her body and trailing on the floor behind her. Mercy slumped to the floor and started to weep. She was leaning with her back against the wall and had her knees drawn up near her chin. There was a torn condom packet on the floor in front of her. The tears continued to flow as she rumpled her hair and half-formed thoughts coursed through her mind. Her world was crumpling and she didn't know what to do about it. Seeing her so distraught, Benjamin tried to comfort her by placing an arm on her shoulder, but she slapped him. He drew back and decided to give her some time to calm down. Mercy continued to cry. Should she tell their mother? What would she think? The bad news might damage her mother's health irreparably and that would be more trouble for her.

What have I ever done to you that you should treat me this way?

Please Mercy. Let's not talk about this now. Please forgive me, I will make this up to you.

Are you still thrilled by cunt after all these years? My own sister? You men have no shame. What is it that I failed to give you? Don't you have any sense of decency? Do you know how despicable what you've done is?

Please forgive me. It's the devil's work.

Shut up.

Let's go to our room. Please, it's very late now.

Look I don't know. I don't know anything anymore. I'm really confused. This thing has fucked me up. I don't know what to do. Who can I trust? I can't trust my husband or my own sister. The world has turned upside-down. Oh, I am finished. I have been ruined. I wouldn't have believed even my enemy could ever do this to me.

More tears flowed down Mercy's cheeks, but she was beginning to get an inkling of her next line of action.

Please let's go to our room.

Will you leave me alone and let me think? You go and let me stay and think here.

Benjamin waited a few moments before leaving the room and walking down the passageway to the matrimonial bedroom. Mercy sat on the floor in Mandy's room wracking her brain for a way out. She decided that she wouldn't tell her mother just yet, to avoid worsening her mother's health. She would send Mandy away to live with their maternal uncle. Their uncle lived three hundred miles north, and she felt that was sufficient distance from her wayward sister to provide herself enough time to heal. But she hadn't decided what she was going to do about Benjamin. She had no clue.

The following morning, Mandy packed her belongings and left the mansion for her maternal uncle's place up north. Benjamin had been trying to find a way to tell her that he would send her some money, but it was far too risky after the previous night's incident. Mandy's face was swollen from weeping and she seemed lost in the haze of her own private world.

Mercy moved to take control of the household and Benjamin felt as if he were a stranger in his own home. For weeks, he tried avoiding his wife and did all he could not to annoy her. Marilyn began to take a more active part in the kitchen as Mercy's pregnancy began to wear her down more and more. Her due date was in a month's time. Benjamin needed his most positive frame of mind to attend to his wife's needs, which weren't many. He was glad that he now had more time to his own devices.

Benjamin started to spend more time in the kitchen on the pretext that he wanted to learn how to take care of Mercy better. She didn't object. He and Marilyn spent hours alone in the kitchen preparing meals and doing other household chores. He got to be more friendly with her even though he was much older than she. She was only nineteen but looked older. She didn't appear tough, and being older and more experienced, he felt he could handle her. One evening, as they were preparing the evening meal he slapped her behind. When she turned around, he winked at her.

What is it?

I've a lovely present for you.

What is it?

I will show you later.

Benjamin looked for signs to see if she was familiar with his pick-up line, but she didn't seem to be. It appeared as if Mandy had not revealed a word to her, so he stuck to his line.

When?

Tonight?

Why not now?

I want it to be a secret between us. Can you keep a secret?

Why not, I'm not a little girl.

I bet you are.

No, I'm not.

Yes you are.

No, I'm not.

I bet you are.

Oh come off it what's the deal?

Tonight, I will give you the most beautiful gift you've ever been given.

Why not now?

I've told you to be patient. Patience is a sign of maturity. In many situations in life, patience is a deciding factor and this is one of those kinds of situations. Tonight, my dear, you will receive your present and you shall be forever be grateful to me. Wait for me in your room at around midnight and I shall surprise you beyond your wildest imagination. Only be patient and play it cool.

They finished making the evening meal of pap, tomato stew, and grilled fish. Marilyn dished out Mercy's share, which she set on a tray and took up to her. Benjamin sat on a chair by the kitchen table and ate alone. Marilyn returned downstairs and served herself some food, which she carried to lounge so that she could watch television while eating. It was safer for them to be apart so that if Mercy decided to come downstairs, she wouldn't suspect anything. Benjamin finished his meal and tossed his plate into the sink and then went upstairs to Mercy. Their relationship had been strained ever since he was caught out, and the pregnancy seemed to have made her even more testy.

How are you feeling my darling?

Ok; and you?

I'm great. Did you enjoy the meal?

No.

What do you like eating?

Mango and eggs.

Mango and eggs? That's a strange combination, but it sounds good for breakfast. Why don't you wait till morning, and then I'll make it for you for breakfast.

I want it for dinner.

I'll make it for you for dinner tomorrow night darling. I promise.

Benjamin settled his palm on Mercy bulging belly and rubbed it gently. Then he put his ear on her belly to see if he could hear the the baby kicking, but heard nothing.

In one month, all this will all be over and you'll be able to get on with your life.

I hope so. But then who would look after the baby?

You and I of course. We'll do it together.

That's what you men always say, but as soon as the baby starts to cry in the middle of night, you'll take off to the guest room or wherever. It's the same story everywhere.

I'm different.

We'll see about that.

This is our first child together and I want to be around to be a father. I can't let the burden rest on you alone. That's impossible. We're in this together darling.

Oh I have aches all over my body.

Would you like a massage?

Yes please, rub my shoulders for me. Careful; don't put too much pressure on my belly.

Don't worry, I will be careful darling.

Can you rub my feet too?

No problem. How about like this? Do you feel better?

Benjamin continued to stroke Mercy's feet. After a few more minutes, he turned his attention once again to her shoulders. He was beginning to fancy his own skills as a masseur.

How are you feeling now?

Tired.

You must try and get some sleep my dear to keep your strength up. Let's sleep early tonight. I'm exhausted too.

Mercy didn't offer reply but merely shut her eyes and took a deep breath. She was already in her nightdress and didn't have to change. Benjamin stood up to change into the shorts he wore to bed and an old t-shirt. He also seized the opportunity to put an expensive gold chain he had bought for Marilyn inside the pocket of a jacket that hung at one end of his wardrobe. He returned to bed and lay beside Mercy. All he had to do now was wait for a few hours and then make his escape. It was a restless period of waiting. He kept tossing and turning.

Ever since Mercy had caught him with her sister, things had changed between them. It wasn't that she displayed any open hostility. She just seemed withdrawn. Her failure to vent her anger on him made him feel slightly guilty. He was also uncertain about her game plan. He had no idea of what action she would take as a result of his wrong-doing. But he preferred not to dwell on such thoughts.

He tried to think of being with Marilyn. Would the adventure be as fulfilling as the one he had had with Mandy? Would she be more than just a mere a fleshpot and open up the corridors of his mind and emotional landscape that had been filling up dust and cobwebs? This seemed most unlikely. But he needed her presence to redress the equilibrium that had been upset by the ejection of Mandy. He needed to regain that element of risk to sharpen the contrasts in his life again.

Some would call Benjamin's cheating right in the marital home with Mercy at home self-destructive behavior. But to Benjamin, it was essential psychotherapy. Risk, danger, death, and life stood side-by-side in a seamless continuity.

He tried to imagine the color of the nightgown or t-shirt Marilyn would be wearing. Would she be wearing something made of satin or would she have on something in silk? Would she have on panties or would she be naked? Would she be reading a bodycare magazine or would it be a music ragsheet? Would she give him trouble convincing her to have sex and tell him to wait until another time, or would she just give in to him as her sister did? They came from the same womb, didn't they?

He thought about and debated within himself a thousand angles that their impending encounter could assume. The strain in his crotch was getting quite uncomfortable. He urgently needed relief. He turned to look at his wife, who seemed to be asleep. Should he caress her body and try to get her aroused? Would she be in the mood? He couldn't tell and thought it was better not to take the risk. Two hours had passed, but still it wasn't time to visit Marilyn. He wished time would evaporate so he could do what he had to do. His pulse raced as his lust and impatience increased. He was at the precipice of risk, but the waiting seemed interminable. He looked at Mercy one more time to assure himself that she was sleeping and then crept out of bed and headed for the spot in his wardrobe where he had stashed the gold chain. After a few moments fumbling in the dark, he found the right pocket and brought out the exquisite piece of jewelry. He hoped it would have a magical effect on Marilyn.

Barefoot, he made for the door as quietly as possible. At the door, he turned around once more. Satisfied that Mercy was still asleep, he turned the knob slowly, upset to hear it squeak. His heart rate increased, but he liked the mounting feeling of danger. He slipped through the door and headed down the passageway sticking to the left-hand side where Marilyn's door was located. Her door was even closer to theirs than Mandy's had been. When he reached it, he hurriedly twisted the knob to let himself in and found that it was locked. He cursed under his breath. How could she have been stupid to lock the door? He had told her repeatedly not to lock it when she was ready to sleep. What sort of game was she up to? Would she disappoint him? What kind of crap was this? Fuck! Should he knock on her door?

With a mix of desperation, lust, and momentary insanity, he knocked a few times with sharp, urgent knocks. He waited just a few seconds before knocking again. Hearing no movement within, he tried again and then put his ear against the door to figure out whether Marilyn was stirring. He cursed beneath his breath. What kind of luck is this? How could she do this to him after all his groundwork? Was this the new sort of game youngsters of her age played with men? He was totally confused. He wanted to call her name loudly and but held himself back. After what seemed like an interminable period he heard a key turn and the door opened slightly. Marilyn appeared through the crack with look of bafflement. She seemed reluctant to let him in.

What do you want?

Have you forgotten our date?

What date?

I'm supposed to bring a present to you this night remember?

Where is the present?

Let me come in. I can't give it to you here.

Marilyn widened the crack of the door just enough to let him squeeze through, but she stood far from the bed and there wasn't a hint of submissiveness in her frame. Her elusiveness confused Benjamin even more. Her bedroom had the same stark décor as Mandy's. Pink walls, a ceiling fan that had gold-plated trimmings, a couple of dressers, a wall mirror, a single inbuilt wardrobe, a couple of upright chairs and a fake Persian rug at the middle of the room.

What sort of game are you playing? I thought you were a mature girl?

I don't understand you. What do you mean?

I told you to leave your door open tonight and now you have me knocking like a madman. Why did you lock it? Tell me why?

I forgot.

That is not good enough. We had a deal. I told you I would visit you this night and that you should leave your door unlocked.

I am used to sleeping with my door locked.

Do you want to see the present I bought for you or not?

Please let me see.

What would you give me in return?

Let me see first if I like it.

I am sure you would like it.

Let me see.

Won't you give me a little kiss first?

No.

You're such a hard-hearted girl.

That's not so.

Just then, Mercy appeared through the door.

What are you doing here Benjamin? So you also want to sleep with Marilyn after you have slept with Mandy?

No I was only talking to her.

Talking to her at this time of the night? You're a shameless man. I regret the day I married you.

Nothing happened. I promise you.

But what are you doing here at this unholy hour? You want to ruin the girl's life? Is that what you want to do after you have finished with Mandy? You want to sleep with all of my sisters? Is that what you want?

No! It's not like that Mercy.

What is it like then, you shameless bastard? You have no self-control. You do your thinking with your cock. Either you will kill me in this house or I'll kill you.

Let's not make a mountain out of a mole hill. Nothing happened and nothing was going to happen. I promise you.

That's a lie. It is only because I came in that nothing happened. I noticed how restless you were on the bed. Tossing and turning as if you had ants in your pants. So this is what you've been planning. No woman can ever satisfy you. Why did you get married then? You're a bitch. That what's you are! A whore of a man. You're a sick dog. You shouldn't live among human beings because you defile everything. Marilyn, tomorrow I'm sending you to our uncle where Mandy is staying. I don't think it would be safe for you in this house. You hear me? Get your things ready and tomorrow you will leave for uncle Tamide's place up north.

All right.

Mercy, please don't get upset because of your condition. Nothing happened I assure you.

Shut up! The last time I kept quiet and didn't tell anyone what you had done, thinking it was a one-off mistake. Now I see you're just a cheap dog. I will let everyone know the kind of man you are. Benjamin Pancho what sort of man are you? Can you go so low as to be sleeping with your wife's sister? Of all the women in the world, why is it that it's my sisters you find attractive? What is it about you that draws you to them? Are you engaged in some kind of ritual and trying to use their blood for money? Is that what you are trying to do Benjamin Pancho?

Please don't talk like that. Nothing happened and nothing will. I promise.

But what are you doing here at this time of the night?

I only came for a brief chat about something.

Brief chat about what? Tell me?

It is only a small matter.

See? You can't tell me you shameless liar. I would ruin your name in this town before you ruin my sisters. If you want to take me down, I will take you down with me.

Please Mercy you know you're due to deliver any time. Don't aggravate your condition.

You're the one aggravating my condition. You're are the one ruining my life and giving me problems. I lose sleep because I'm worried that you're trying to leave my bed at night to fuck my sister. What kind of man are you Benjamin Pancho? What have I gotten myself into? I'm not going to take it lightly with you this time. Everyone in this town will know the sort of man you are.

What sort of man I am? What have I done wrong this time? I didn't do anything and you are getting angry with me.

You are such a liar. Tell me what are you doing in Marilyn's bedroom at this hour? Is that how a real man behaves? Why did you sneak out the way you did, like a thief? You think I didn't see you? I saw everything. I saw when you went to the wardrobe and brought something out. I don't know what it is, but I saw you take something and then walk slowly to the door like a cat about to catch a mouse. Why were you being so sneaky if your intentions were honorable? Look at yourself . . . you aren't even wearing slippers so that you wouldn't make a noise. Look at you sweating now. Why are you sweating? What is making you sweat if not the blatant lies you are telling? Look, I saw everything. You thought I was asleep. You can't be trusted.

Mercy burst into tears. Benjamin put his arm around her shoulders and tried to comfort her but she brushed him off. He stood nonplussed, not knowing what to do next. Marilyn, who had been watching all along, had her back to the wall.

Please Mercy, let's go to our bedroom and not give the devil a chance.

You are the devil himself.

How can you say such a thing?

I repeat it. Yyou are the devil himself.

No, don't say that. It's not fair. I didn't do anything.

Mercy shed some more tears, but eventually went back to the matrimonial bedroom. Benjamin knew it was best not to sleep beside her that night and went downstairs to lie on a sofa in the main lounge. He was wet with perspiration but glad that the worst seemed to be over. Soon, waves of mosquitoes started to bother him. He knew he wouldn't be able to sleep. He endeavored to carry out a postmortem of the night's proceedings. Where had he gone wrong? What moves did he take that shouldn't have been taken? How could he go about perfecting his act? He felt no remorse about what he had done. Instead, he felt slightly angry and disappointed that his plans had not gone well.

Marilyn was a major culprit. She was supposed to have left her door open but the dim-witted girl locked it. He must have aroused Mercy's suspicions by his flurry of knocks. That was part of what undid him. If only he had disappeared quickly into Marilyn's bedroom, Mercy would not have known where he had gone within the mansion. He could have told a dozen lies about where he had been if she bothered to ask. What a shit the evening had been.

Perhaps his strategy was wrong. He must have had to do more to allay Mercy's ingrained suspicions. He should have done more to win back her trust. But hadn't he done enough by giving her an elaborate massage? Hadn't he shown her enough empathy? Had he already exhausted all the options available to him? If he were aloof in his manner, then she would have reason to observe him more closely. Now that he had shown her empathy, she still watched him. When would she forget about the experience with Mandy so that they could both live in peace? He didn't want to continue to like a stranger and a thief in his own home just because of a couple of mistakes he had made. Mistakes do occur, but it was necessary to forge ahead and not dwell upon them. Hadn't he done everything to provide her material needs? Wasn't that achievement enough to provide him with just a bit of leeway to allow him to cater to his urges? She was just an ungrateful bitch. He shouldn't have married her. He should begin to look into the possibility of breaking up their burdensome union. Yes that was what he would do. He would send her packing and find someone else.

Mercy could not sleep the entire night. She lay crying on her bed until dawn. The drumming and handclapping from the white garment church down the street provided no comfort. But she decided to report Benjamin's latest escapade to the elders of the church. Perhaps being religious, they would be able to talk some sense into him. At seven o'clock, she managed to drag herself to the church, which was open at all hours. Elders, various officials, volunteers of all cadres, and vagrants drifted in and out of the premises anytime. The work of the church was one without end. When Mercy walked through the gates, it was clear that all was not well with her. She asked a female volunteer if she could see the committee of elders urgently.

It is a bit early. I think they are still deep in prayer.

Please tell them it is Mercy Pancho. They all know me and I'm sure they would want to see me because it is very urgent.

I'll see what I can do.

The female volunteer wore a simple, grey, ankle-length skirt with a white blouse that looked like a chorister's uniform. Mercy kept apace until they got near the altar, when the volunteer indicated that she should wait. The volunteer turned and disappeared through a side door to the right, from which a dark blue curtain hung. Mercy was feeling very exhausted and so leaned on the headrest of a bench. It wasn't comfortable, so she hoped she would be admitted soon. After a couple of minutes, the volunteer re-emerged and said that she could go in through the side door. Mercy dragged herself along with a hand on her jutting belly.

When she reached the door, she shoved the blue curtain aside and waited to see the faces of those in the little room: elder Jacob, elder Matthew, and elder Michael. She bent her knees slightly in greeting and Jacob got up from his seat and ran to her telling her to sit and make herself comfortable.

How are you?

I am well sir.

Please feel at home. You know is your home.

Michael asked,

What can we do for you?

A lot of things sir. I have come to see you because I don't want any trouble.

Yes, we know you are not a troublesome woman.

Mercy burst into tears. Michael stood at her shoulder consoling her.

Don't cry my dear woman all will be well.

I don't know sir. I am tired.

What is it my dear woman asked Jacob.

It is my husband. I am tired of him.

Benjamin? interjected Matthew.

Yes. I am just tired.

What has he done? asked Jacob.

He has been sleeping with my sisters.

That can't be true! said Jacob.

It is sir. I have caught him red-handed twice. How much can a woman take? I have had to chase Mandy and Marilyn away so that they won't be within easy reach. I have done all I can to make him happy. I am even expecting his first child next month, and see how he treats me! He wants to kill me, but before he does, I'll leave him. Let him find another woman with sisters he can sleep with. This isn't meant to be my lot in life. It can't be. I am a spiritual person and my morals are different from his. I mean, why did he marry in the first place if he knew he would be sleeping with his wife's sisters? What kind of culture allows that? I am tired and I want to leave him before he kills me.

Jacob looked at his two colleagues for some sort of approval before he began:

My child. We know you are aggrieved, but you mustn't take matters into your own hands. We mustn't allow the devil to take control of our lives. Isn't that so?

Yes said Michael and Matthew jointly.

We must do things in a way that is entirely free of the devil's involvement. I am not denying that Benjamin did the things you said he did, but we have to talk to him first and find out what went wrong. We have to make sure he is in his right senses and that he is not been used by the devil because, my dear child, the devil is very powerful. Yes, very powerful indeed. So, we must ensure that we do not play into the devil's hands. Marriage is a holy thing. People tend to forget that, and that is why you see so many cases of people getting married today and divorced tomorrow. You see, such people do not know what marriage entails. They think it's a joke and that you can just shop for a spouse get divorced whenever convenient. I don't know what the world is turning to. The world is being taken over by jokers and scoundrels and it our duty to resist the power of their evil influence. We must put them to shame at every opportunity we get, or the whole world is doomed. So, my child, that is why I say we must tread carefully so that we do not fall into the hands of the devil.

You see there are devil-made craters all around us and it is our duty to remain vigilant so we don't fall into them. Otherwise, we will not be able realize our destinies in this life. So dry your tears my child and think of the strategies you must employ to see that the devil does not gain power over your household. I am not talking about a creature with horns and a tail. The devil might be working through husband, your sister, or your best friend, or even your mother.

So, my child, that is why I am urging you to look inward and search yourself for a better solution to this crisis. You see, you don't know what you're dealing with. Many women would die for a mere fraction of what you've got. The devil may attempt to attack you from any angle and at any time. You must be prepared to defend you home and protect its integrity. Men are like babies and Benjamin is a child; you must treat him as such. You must give him room to put to right his wrongs. But if you get heavy-handed with him, he might just run away and you would lose him finally. So my advice is that we tread carefully and give him some time to see the wrongfulness of his ways. You have to be patient. In good time, we will summon him and talk to him as men should. Until then, my child, I want you to return home and wait for further instructions from us. Please don't do anything rash. That would only make matters worse. So, my child, return to your home now and keep your peace.

Jacob walked Mercy to the gate. Mercy dragged herself home not feeling entirely satisfied with the elder's counsel, but she knew she didn't have the strength to fight Benjamin just yet. She ought to be saving her remaining energy for the birth of her child. That should be her priority. But what was she to do with such a wayward man for a husband? After she'd had her baby, she would find a way to dish him a really low blow. She shouldn't have expected the elders of the church to provide her with the support she needed. Benjamin had a special relationship with them that many within their congregation could never hope to have. He was a generous supporter of their programs and even sponsored some of the members of the church, including the church elders, to undertake theological courses at various religious establishments. He was one member they could not afford to lose.

The elders decided to broach the news of Mercy visit in the lightest of terms. They wouldn't disclose that she had accused him of sleeping with her sisters. It was a scandal they wanted no part of. They decided that the best way to approach the matter was to advise Benjamin to try and make his wife happy so that she doesn't suffer a miscarriage. Mercy's health and comfort mustn't be jeopardized for any reason, and on that score, it was up to him to be a responsible husband. When they gave the mild advice regarding the nature of his conduct as a husband, Benjamin repaid their considerate entreaties with gifts of rice, tea and coffee, a sack of potatoes, gallons of vegetable oil, a large bag of salt, corn flour, and large tins of powdered milk. They responded to his overwhelming generosity by offering special prayers of his behalf.

Mercy gave birth to a healthy baby girl. She wasn't as delighted as she ought to have been because Benjamin had hoped for boy; he was a man with traditional aspirations. Even after she regained her strength, taking care of the household was a rather heavy burden for Mercy without her sisters' assistance.

Benjamin had become increasingly frustrated with Mandy and Marilyn being gone. He didn't know what to do with himself as days and weeks passed. He felt dull and without purpose. But he did his best to disguise his true emotions. The only joy in his life was his baby Humbi who grew more beautiful with each passing day. He loved to carry her while her mother was downstairs making meals and doing other chores. He would spend time cooing and singing to his beautiful baby. Humbi delighted him; he vowed to protect her from a hurt-filled world.

At the same time, Benjamin started to have troubling feelings for Humbi. He would stroke her genitals when changing her diapers. He stopped when she cried or sensed that he was causing her discomfort. His pulse increased anytime he carried the baby in his arms ever since he began stroking her genitals.

Mercy grew worried when she noticed that Humbi had a stubborn diaper rash. Benjamin wasn't worried because he knew virtually nothing about baby care and health. He had began to see Humbi as a distinct individual in her own right and took to taking her into the bathroom to stroke her with his cock. He couldn't get enough of his latest preoccupation and started to indulge in it at every available opportunity. He avoided stroking Humbi with his dick on the matrimonial bed but took her instead into the bathroom where he removed his shorts and placed the baby on the wash stand while he satisfied himself with her. This threw him into paroxysms of insanity as well as euphoria. It was a feeling better than his lust for his wife's sisters.

His luck ran out at five thirty one evening when Mercy came up from downstairs into the bedroom and didn't see Benjamin and Humbi. She opened the bathroom door and saw her husband standing without his shorts with his erect penis over her baby, who was lying in the wash stand. She wanted to scream, but her husband struck her with his fist on her shoulder. The blow almost hurled her out of the bathroom. She was doubly stunned. Benjamin struck as a result of the frustration of being caught rather than from the apprehension of Mercy alerting neighbors with her screams. He felt thwarted that she had caught him out again.

Give me my baby you mad man!

Take her.

Bastard. You will rot in hell. It's over. I am leaving this house today. I know a curse has been placed here. No good thing can come from here.

Benjamin did not try to stop her as she packed her baby's essentials. Somehow, he knew he would get over the setback. After all, he had wrestled with the cult of the dead and eventually won his liberty. What could be more gruesome than that ordeal? He had seen the visage of death and it had invited him for a nice cup of coffee. How about that as a sign of toughness? It would be Mercy's word against his. With money, truth can be bought, manufactured, and conjured out of thin air. He would see how Mercy would convince the world about what he had done. He would claim that she had lost her mind and had been having severe mental health problems for sometime but that he had kept it secret in the hope that she would get better. But alas, now she is claiming that he fucked his own daughter. What could be more absurd?

That was the way he intended to present his case. He was glad that he still had steely resolve lodged deep within his heart. That was what had brought him his great wealth. It was what had enabled him to continue with his life after his life-threatening brush with the cult of the dead. Fuck her, fuck her family, fuck her sisters too. He could do without their useless load of shit. They could all go to hell for all he cared. He would make another life without them and they would be surprised to see that he would succeed.

Rumors of Benjamin's incest spread around town. But no one had the opportunity to confront him because he was rarely seen. He had become such an inverterate recluse so long ago that many people had forgotten what he looked like. Facts, rumors, and falsehoods about Benjamin had created a vast mythological figure that transcended the divisions between myth and reality. This act of discursive transcendence achieved the result of absolving him from the responsibilities of common, earth-bound moralities. His enormous material resources had almost completely made him a creature beyond good and evil.

Such was the intricacy of Benjamin Pancho's legend that when he was killed in a sudden car crash three months after he was caught molesting his baby, no one believed he was dead. He hadn't been seen for ages and it was never clear whether he was still alive. No one was sure whether the categories of life and death even applied to him. He seemed to traverse both categories like a mythical cat that lived in the womb of night.

The legend of Benjamin Pancho did not die. His former hangers-on and henchmen spread it far and wide. In his old neighborhood, the likes of Chidi kept stoking the fire of the legend. Myth and reality became interchangeable. On the day Chidi heard of Benjamin's death, Ade Bantan dashed into the apartment he shared with Enitan and her siblings.

Have you heard?

What?

Benjamin Pancho, the richest man in the area is dead.

How did he die?

We don't know yet. There are many stories. Some say he kept a secret snake in his mansion that acted as his guardian, and someone inadvertently killed it. When Benjamin saw the snake had been killed, he moaned heavily and said a terrible thing had occurred, and then fell down and died. Others say he entered into a secret cult where he made a promise to produce the blood of his wife and children for sacrificial offerings within the cult in exchange for great wealth. They say he failed to keep his side of the bargain and the cult took away his soul. But others say he was now living in exile in Chile. We don't know all the details yet but we may never see Benjamin Pancho again.

Interesting, said Ade Bantan.

Yes it is. He was the most impressive man in this godforsaken town. He made a difference and knew how spend money. He was a great man. The parties he threw were the stuff of legend. The chicks wore diamond studded slippers to his gigs. Trailer-load of cows were slaughtered each and every time; their blood ran through the street for days. The neighborhood dogs grew fat lapping up flowing bulls' gore. All the beggars would line up around the his gates singing his praises and he would throw wads and wads of cash that some of them floated into the gutters and got washed away by the flood and muck. The man was simply unbelievable. All the kids are saying they want to be like Benjamin Pancho. Their parents pray that their kids turn out to be another Benjamin Pancho. The girls fantasize about falling in love with someone like Benjamin Pancho. Bro, it seems Pancho is the man to be. The man changed lives. He made a difference and that is what our society needs. We need men who care for the sick, the poor, and the dejected. We need people like Benjamin Pancho to turn our lives around.

But you've just said he joined a cult that traded in human blood.

That's a rumor. Plain hearsay. His detractors spread a lot of lies about him because they are jealous of his wealth and because they are envious that they would never be capable of what he did.

Have you ever met this man or spoken to him?

No, but I saw him once many years ago being driven in a car. His car was in a convoy, a fleet of about forty cars. Amazing.

Yes it is really amazing. So what's going to happen to his supposedly vast wealth?

The good thing is most of it is stashed away in foreign lands, so it is out of the reach of corrupt politicians who have been scheming to get their hands on it. You see even the politicians grudgingly acknowledge his greatness. They really don't want to, but they have to, because the simple fact of the matter is that he changed many, many lives. He is my personal hero and he motivates me to do something with my life. Even though I'm sleeping on balconies today, there is hope for tomorrow. He came from virtually nothing and turned his life around. He is an absolute genius and I want to try and be like him. The white garment church will be holding festivals to commemorate his earthly life. They too do not believe that he is dead. They say he his going through a period of transition to ascend to a higher plane of existence. A great man is never without controversy. Benjamin Pancho even with all his faults was a great man.

Ade Bantan knew there was no point arguing with Chidi about Benjamin Pancho's qualities as a man. They came from two different worlds in that regard. Benjamin Pancho's life had no meaning for Ade Bantan. He merely heard legendary tales of his doings and omissions without paying them undue attention. He despised the fact that he was thrust into the position of having to listen to the tales. He had far more pressing commitments to attend to. He had to put together a portfolio of paintings to demonstrate to the art world that he was still alive. But how could he accomplish this when his imagination seemed to have deserted him and when he hadn't the slightest will to create?

Pressure to marry Enitan kept mounting upon Ade Bantan; everyone expected it. They had been lovers for long enough. She kept pressuring him to commence a program of pre-marital counseling in preparation for their big day. There was also the nagging problem of his finances. He hadn't been making any money and was really eating deep into his savings. He had nothing to look forward to on many fronts.

People like Benjamin Pancho could not be bothered with art unless it had some material value attached. For instance, could the art works be used in secret rituals? Would they be suitable for the decoration of hidden shrines in which only the initiated are admitted? That was the only wavelength the likes of Benjamin Pancho understood in relation to art. Ade Bantan did not even bother to come up with ideas to pitch to his ilk. But he knew some artists who eagerly sought such characters. They made semi-commissioned artifacts for secret shrines that only a handful of people would enter. They made drums for rituals of drunken revelry. They made wraps of tie-dyed material. Such artists were sometimes allowed to sit around in such drunken orgies and routinely dished insults.

Ade Bantan did not have the heart to go that route. But he hadn't the heart to go down any other route either. Each day, all that weighed on his mind was how he would produce enough paintings for at least a group exhibition. The fact that he wasn't making any effort made his inertia even more painful. He had lied to Enitan that he had enough completed work for the foreign exhibitions he was planning. But he had nothing in store. Sooner or later, the truth would be revealed and he would have to deal with the consequences. Until then, he resolved to spend his time lying on Enitan's couch.

Toscin came into the living room to iron the clothes she intended to wear. She sat on the floor in front of the television and stereo as she always did when she had ironing to do. For the first time, Ade Bantan took notice of her in a different sort of way. The tall young woman was wearing a red sleeveless t-shirt that had black stripes. As Enitan had so long ago, Toscin was wearing a plaid micro miniskirt. Her legs were spread apart before her and she ironed her clothes between them. It was all right to do that since she had her back to him. Her micro mini had slipped further down at her back so Ade Bantan could see her eye-catching white g-string. It created a powerful effect on him. Her lovely lithe back made deliberate, slow movements as her arms ironed clothes on the floor between her legs.

Toscin was unaware of the impact her back, g-string, and spread legs made on AdeBantan. She wouldn't have thought such sights would throw the usual order of his emotions and day into disarray. After all, her sister, whom he was about to marry, also had a stunning figure. She could never imagine her potential in-law succumbing to common temptations of the flesh. This was how Toscin would have thought about the matter, but the reality was quite the opposite.

What would be the consequences if Ade Bantan attempted to fuck Toscin? If he succeeded, a new chemical element would be thrown into the equation that was bound to upset everything. If he failed, he would have to live with the horrible thought of Toscin disclosing to Enitan what he had done to her sister. Then everything would be lost; the meager circumference of his reputation, the warmth and friendship of a family that had wholeheartedly welcomed him and finally the acceptance of friends and the community and respect from them. This was all he stood to lose from indulging in a few risky moments of fleshly pleasures. This was all he stood to destroy if he succumbed to the myopic thinking of his cock. No it didn't amount to thinking of the cock.

Instead, it was precisely a delirium of the cock that seized every part of his body. At the heart of this delirium was the familiar tussle between simplicity and complexity. Society had to run along simple, functional lines. Complexity was to be avoided when it didn't lead to generalized cohesion of the social body. So, you did not give in to the urge to fuck your lover's sister unless you both subscribed to the libertine's philosophy of pleasure and could tolerate the ostracism.

The compulsion to fuck your wife's sister is a complicated and perhaps also a confused desire for complexity. It is a fervent attempt to escape the ministrations and the restrictions of the humdrum. It is also a mad craving for the joys of excess and expenditure. The civilized world has not only denigrated counterculture notions of excess and expenditure, it has succeeded in expunging them from the materiality of everyday life. So, it has been deemed respectable to restrict the delirium of the cock to within strict matrimonial borders. Any form of penal delirium that exceeds the borders of matrimony is stigmatized as a sign of excess, a form of selfish delirium that ought to be stamped out immediately at its roots.

Ade Bantan knew that despite the naturalness of his thinking about the nature of human excess, it was a marginal way of thinking. He would have his haunches splayed and fed to the dogs if he yielded to his most natural urges. He would be deemed insane and carted off to the nuthouse and have the key to his cell thrown to the bottom of the sea. There he would remain, a broken and forgotten man, as his hair got tangled on the ceiling and his nails grew through the bars of his cell. Toscin, who had been the unwitting source of so much philosophizing, finished her ironing and got up with a generous show of naked limb and with her delirium-inducing g-string still prominently exposed.

Ade Bantan shut his eyes and tried to clear his head. He could hear Mama Osaze singing to her baby. He could hear the door to Chidi's mother's apartment banging. The sounds from the streets rose up to him and filled up his head. In those conditions, it was difficult to clear his head. He felt tired but he couldn't sleep. What would people think if they came into the living room and saw him sleeping at that time of the day? His girlfriend was slaving away at work while he sat on his arse and engaged in protracted bouts of internal whining?

Already Enitan was at pains to constantly remind people that Ade Bantan was a highly accomplished artist who had a number of exhibitions lined up in foreign countries. She would mention that they were in the process of relocating abroad where the market was better for his art. They intended to spend half the year abroad and the other half here at home. She would also like to have their babies overseas because the conditions were much better over there. Enitan had elaborate dreams of their future together but he couldn't even provide the most insignificant brush strokes to her master plan regarding the construction of their ostensibly joint future together. She simply held him by the hand and led him down a corridor of mists.

Ade Bantan admired Enitan's courage, her optimism in making something out of mists and numerous uncertainties. She seemed not to quite understand the concept of uncertainty. In her world, direct action was all that made sense and had tangible value. That was why she kept pushing to begin pre-marital counseling; so they could accomplish the ultimate materialization of her dream of a joint future. Ade

Bantan, on the other hand, was more attracted to the realities of mists, the way they slowly unraveled their labyrinthine arguments, the way they suggested the conditions for their truths in very subtle ways, and the way they patiently articulated the silence of their words. That was the kind of world he understood and this fundamental difference between them was the epitome of the ongoing debate on the relations between simplicity and complexity.

Ade Bantan was still lying on the couch when Ulmanmadu, a distant relative of Enitan, entered the living room.

How are you my potential in-law? offering Ade Bantan his hand to shake.

Fine thank you. How are you doing?

Hustling as ever. You know you can't get out of the hustle. The hustle is what makes life go round.

Yeah that is true. So what brings you to our area.

I just wanted to see how my potential in-law is doing and to make sure my sisters are treating you well. Toscin! Toscin!

Toscin emerged from the corridor with a puzzled expression on her face.

Are you treating our in-law well? Are you doing all you can to make him happy? I hope you're not giving him any trouble?

We are doing our best.

Good. I'll see you later.

They look after me well.

And that is why we need to talk. If my sisters are treating
you as well as you say, then it means our family is a good one.
It is a family any man should be happy to marry into and we
must make haste because other men are lurking around
awaiting their chance. You see, in our culture, the younger
ones cannot marry unless the older one clear the way. I hope
you get my point. Time is passing, and so we must do what
we have to do while we can. You see, no one must know I
am talking to you now. I have come on my own. No one sent
me. Nonetheless, I represent the thinking men in our family.
I am also very fond of you. You seem to be a gentle, loving
man who has no trouble with anyone. That is how life should
be lived. I have a strong feeling that you know how to live life
and of course I want the best for my sister. But as I have said,
we must do everything in time and at the right time. We
mustn't leave what we can do today until tomorrow. I hope
you get my point. Enitan is no longer a small girl. Her
agemates by now have three or four kids and as it is, she
doesn't even have one. This is not good and I personally want
that to change. As I have told you, no one sent me to you and
I am here of my own volition. But at the same time, my line
of thought is not an usual one within the family. As I said, I
represent the right thinking men. As you know, every family,
including some of the best like our own, has its own share of
problems, black sheep and arseholes and bitches. But the
right thinking men in our own family are in the majority. We
are also a very proud family. I am unusual because I am a
humble person. None of them would approach you as I am
doing now because they would see it as being beneath their

dignity. I hope you're getting the point I'm making. We know our worth as a family and we know the worth of our women. Our women are very good as you, yourself, have said. They are kind, loving, gentle, and know how to take care of men. Is this not so? Good. But we as men must also begin to show the right level of appreciation for these wonderful women. We must not let them remain on the market too long because we don't want to unduly expose them to the dangers of wolves. In fact, it is the general opinion that they should not in anyway be exposed to the wolves. We must do all we can to ensure they are piloted into the right houses. I hope you are getting the point I am making. Also, Enitan's case warrants my intervention because of her very special position in the family. She is not only a sister to our girls but also a mother and a mother should have a good man by her side so that the younger ones can learn from him. Is this not so? Good. I think you fit each other. She is very beautiful and you are not bad looking either. I can't wait to see what your children would look like. Also, I want to tell you a secret. Enitan is hot property in the market. Many men are dying to have her hand and I don't want you to lose her. She is meant for you and she would bring you good luck. You just try and experience so many other good things about her that I can't tell you now because you will say I told you so. Enitan has some hidden good sides that will only be revealed later. They can't be revealed now because some worthless men might take advantage of her. But once she is in your house as your wife, then you will recognize that you have probably married the best queen in the world for you. Believe me, my brother. I'm not giving you shit. If you don't know me well, ask around in the neighborhood. Everyone will tell you that Ulmanmadu is no bullshitter. I don't want to give you shit and don't want you to give Enitan shit. She doesn't deserve it at all because she is a lovely angel. You know she has a lot brothers and they are keen to see her happy; they would die for her. No shit. We would die for that woman. I hear you are starting a job overseas is that true?

I'm trying to work something out.

Please be quick about it so you two can get on with your lives. Time waits for no man and the earlier things are done, the better. Do you know anything about our culture? Do you know how to go about proposing marriage?

A bit.

It is a very exacting process and things have got to go according to plan. You have to send an emissary to us men first. This is not an formal request; it is only a communication divulging a statement of intent. Of course, you have to buy drinks for the occasion. I suggest you should put aside funds for drinks for at least fifty people. You know we are a very large family and Enitan has a lot of friends. This is probably the most important event in her life and all her numerous well-wishers can be expected to be there. So let's just think in terms of fifty people being present. When you arrive with your crew, we shall welcome you and offer you all seats. We shall introduce the key members of our crew, in short our family. You shall introduce yourselves as well. We may also provide you with snacks; kolanuts, bitter kola, eggplant dipped in palm oil, coconut and salt, alligator pepper, and more appetizing whatnot. Just play it cool, there isn't much to it. After the first round of drinks, a delegate from your crew would mention casually that there is a she-goat in our yard that has caught the attention of a member of your crew.

Some of us would feign ignorance and surprise and ask which she-goat is so unfortunate as to have ignited the attention of a member of your crew. You shall mention her name and the she-goat would emerge from one of the bedrooms in the house wearing traditional attire behind a veil of beads on her face. Then she will kneel before all present and say a modest hello to everyone. She will then return into the bedroom to give the men time to confer. There will be a pause in the deliberations as more alcohol is being consumed and general jokes made. The purpose if this visit is to break the ice and to reveal a statement of intent regarding one of the she-goats in our yard. You see, it is not difficult at all, and then things can proceed rapidly from there. So my brother, this is what I have come to tell you. You are my brother and you can expect me by your side always in this matter.

Thank you; I really appreciate it.

Oh, don't let anyone know I came to talk to you. Not Enitan, Sumbo, or Toscin. This is strictly confidential.

Ade Bantan accompanied UImanmadu to the bus stop while Ulmanmadu continued to prattle about many things; the mysterious disappearance and alleged death of Benjamin Pancho being his main topic of interest.

Ade Bantan returned to the apartment and resumed his position of the couch. It was a blistering day. He wondered how he had kept his cool while Ulmanmadu corralled him into a corner. What cheek. He didn't regard him as a friend and the cad had the audacity to preach to him about what is supposed to be a private affair. Who told him he wanted to get married in the first place? He didn't recall declaring such

132

intentions to any member of the family. Was it because he spent days on end lying on Enitan's couch? Did this seemingly harmless activity signify an implicit declaration of intent? He found all of it baffling. How could he have a lout such as Ulmanmadu as an in-law? What would they have in common beyond prowling about pepper soup joints and seedy beer dens? And then, what kind of conversations would they have that didn't dwell on strategies for having affairs with bar girls? He couldn't see any future connection, yet the lout had presumed to inform him on an affair he had wanted to handle solely by himself. But he didn't think the time was right to put him in his place.

Indeed, what gave him the gumption to express such crass suppositions was the fact that he was a couch fly who had made Ulmanmadu's distant relative's living room his resting place. That was it and nothing more. The sun's heat seemed to increase and sweat poured slowly and steadily out of his body. He wished Enitan would arrive from work soon. He was always pleased when she did. On such occasions, they would have ample time to chat, have a joint, and then retire early. As usual, there was no electricity, and it made staying indoors a torture. He was too old to hang around street corners like young men did. He also didn't want to hang out in front of the yard like many men who had been thrown out of the labor market. Such men spent their time gossiping about what such and such a couple did in their apartment. Who had just bought a new pair of shoes. Who got that teenager pregnant, and when last their wives allowed them to sleep with them. He just couldn't sink to that level. It was better to wither away in style and in the privacy of the apartment like some hopeless heroin addict unable to shake off a particularly bad habit.

Enitan returned from work at nine thirty that evening. The electricity still hadn't been restored. Sumbo, Toscin, and Susan were all already in bed, so she tiptoed into the bedroom to remove her clothes and pull out a bed sheet. Ade Bantan was pretending to be asleep, so she didn't come over to give him a kiss as she often did. She came out of the bedroom and then lay on the floor in front of the silent television set. She lay on her stomach with both hands underneath her chin for support.

Having been in darkness for so long, Ade Bantan could make out the contours of her body. He could smell her day-old fragrance from his position on the couch. As his imagination dwelled on the combination of her waning fragrance and quite distinct contours of her body, he started getting an erection. When he was fully hard, he eased himself slowly and quietly from the couch and crept up to Enitan from behind. She didn't hear or notice him until he was directly atop, her which gave her quite a fright.

What are you doing? I thought you were asleep.

Welcome home darling. Missed you.

Missed you too.

You smell great.

Thanks. Have you had dinner?

Yes.

What did you guys have?

Oh the usual boiled plantain and veggies.

Aren't you tired of eating that?

It is healthy food, so I can't complain. So how was work today?

My boss was at me again today. He's just trying to get into my pants and I keep telling him I'm not loose in the arse.

You must tell him to go fuck himself.

I need this job and until I find an alternative, I'll have to tolerate his shit.

Poor you, but I can't blame him. If I were in his shoes, I'd do the same.

Would you?

Of course. I don't suppose you know the effect you have on men.

I don't.

Well let me show you.

Ade Bantan began by kissing Enitan's calves and slowly worked his way through her back and then her shoulders. He kissed her nape, her brows, her nose, inside her ears, and then her eyes. She turned on her back so he could kiss her breasts as well. Patiently, he kissed each of her breasts until she was ready for him. He wasn't done. He put his tongue on her navel and tried to tickle her. She moaned and arched her back. She wanted him all the more. He stroked each of her breasts again and grabbed some cushions from the couch to place beneath her. As he eased himself atop her, she started to moan. Then she suggested they find some place in the yard where they could be by themselves and not have to bother whether her sisters could be listening.

It wasn't a bad idea to have some outdoor sex since there was no electricity, making the neighborhood pitch-dark. Enitan held Ade Bantan by the hand and led him toward the main staircase of the building. The yard seemed silent which meant most people were inside their apartments and rooms. They clutched the walls in order not to bump into things. Only a single small sheet wrapped around Enitan's body. Ade Bantan wore a pair of shorts and nothing else. Slowly, they went down the stairs until they came to the landing. Enitan pulled Ade Bantan behind her and hitched up the sheet. He stripped off his shorts and she bent forward leaning on a step.

It felt delightful to be having sex at such an unusual place. It was airy on the staircase and the element of risk in their activity increased Ade Bantan's arousal. He admired Enitan's imagination for thinking of the spot. While they were at it, the electricity suddenly returned. Its suddenness seemed like flashlights turned upon a pair of thieves or criminals breaking out of a jailhouse. Enitan was very fast in reacting, pushing the sheet down to cover half of her nakedness. Ade Bantan blinked sheepishly as if they had been caught, but no one was around. The sole witness was the naked light bulb that hung at the top of the staircase. He pulled up his shorts and returned with Enitan to the living room. The lights were on and he switched them off. They resumed their lovemaking on the floor, but Enitan had become slightly tense because of their proximity to her sisters, who had always left the bedroom door open.

Darling we can't continue to sleep here.

Yeah you're right. I'll tell Sumbo and the others to sleep in the living room from now on.

That would be great darling. We can have far more privacy then.

But privacy in such circumstances was relative. In the slum, it was still a mystery how large families are made. Sometimes, on Enitan's days off, Ade Bantan would want to make love during the day with the door of the living room shut, but Enitan would refuse, reasoning that it would be obvious to everyone in the building that they were fucking, which would mark them as incorrigible sex maniacs in a yard of religious fanatics. So, within the context of the yard, the concept of privacy was an alien one that was not encouraged. There was no need for an external morality police to enforce regulations relating to sexuality. Instead, the strictures of self-censorship were a much better disciplinary mechanism.

It was a mystery how the likes of Papa and Mama Osaze managed the affairs of sex within their cramped little apartment with four children. Perhaps they hid under their beds so that they won't be seen by their children and this was probably why the sex/guilt/hypocrisy nexus was such a powerful one. Ade Bantan could not fathom how life and sex were possible without the presence of space. Some of the couples lived in single rooms with six or seven children some of whom were teenagers who knew about sex. So when did those couples have sex?

Of course, slum dwellers did have sex, and frequently. Months ago, a woman sat on a rock by the gate crying. She looked rough, as if she hadn't slept for the night and bunched up her wrap between her legs and propped up her chin which was wet with tears and spittle. When asked what was wrong she wasn't keen to offer an answer. She kept crying with tears and spittle dribbling down her face. Eventually, she said her husband bothered her for sex all the time and she was just so thoroughly sick of it. That was a startling revelation.

This was a straight-laced, church-attending family for whom the concept of experimental or outdoor sex would be anathema. This meant all sexual acts were conducted within the cramped sweaty confines of the single room she shared with her husband and eight children. So at what time of the day or night did her bony-arsed husband keep pestering her for sex? For most inhabitants of the yard, such encounters were normal and part of marital life, but Ade Bantan could not figure out how space or the disturbing lack of it figured into the equation.

Enitan had demonstrated that she had a healthy understanding of space by leading him to the pitch-dark staircase for a fuck. That told him that their present living arrangement in a one bedroom apartment couldn't be regarded as permanent as opposed to fathers who sired half a dozen kids in a single room within the space of a decade. Ade Bantan would die of spatial suffocation if that were to be his fate. The only reason he could put up with living in Enitan's apartment now was because of the kindness of her sisters. He was puzzled by how their distinct personalities were able to evolve without the provision of space. Space was like sunlight. Plants need sunlight to thrive. Instead, he saw multitudes, masses of people thriving in dark, sunless spaces without losing in a fundamental way the qualities and features constitute humanity; kindness, generosity, anger, duplicity, considerateness, beauty. The human element was truly resilient.

Perhaps the emergence of a deluge of churches managed to impart the possibilities and significance of hope amid so much squalor, degradation, and scarcity. The emergence of rampant spirituality re-inscribed a primal tussle that framed the entire existential dilemma: good versus evil.

Ade Bantan hoped Enitan would follow through on her promise to get them sleeping in the bedroom instead of the living room. She had started to complain of chest pain, probably as a result of having to sleep each night on the hard bare floor. There were no extra mattresses to cushion her against the hardness.

The following morning, Hankpkaun, a friend of Enitan who lived in the yard, came to inform them of her wedding plans. She would be getting married to an unemployed refrigerator repairman; and it was visible that she was about four months pregnant.

The news Hankpkaun brought intensified Enitan's desire for marriage. All her friends were getting married and soon, she wouldn't fit into their interests and conversation. It would always be my husband did that, my children did this, my in-laws did that. I bought this that and the other for my husband, children, and in-laws. She didn't want to get to the point where her friends abandoned her because she failed to take the supposedly next huge step in life: wedded existence. She had to ensure that she constantly pinched and prodded Ade Bantan to move ahead with her. She had to make sure she got him off the couch he seemed to love more than any other thing. She was also mindful that he was busy forming mental images to paint. But all told, his life wasn't as difficult as hers. All he had to do was to prepare for his exhibitions in

Europe and their marriage. She, on the other hand, had a demanding work schedule, several siblings, many monthly bills to pay, an aged mother, and a vast network of relatives as well as Ade Bantan among her innumerable worries. She was bogged down by her various commitments, but she was tough, a dogged fighter. Wedded life was just another phase of life she had to navigate.

Ade Bantan and Enitan were lying on the mattress in the bedroom when she came in just before she went off to work. The way Hankpkaun had announced her wedding plans stuck in Enitan's mind.

Guess what guys. It's going to happen soon. I am getting married.

Is that so? How lovely my friend. I'm so happy for you. So when is it taking place?

About two months time, so please get ready.

Of course we'll be there, won't we Ade Bantan?

Sure. And how is your intended?

He's doing very well thank you.

Hankpkaun was dressed in a chic, formal way. She had on a black tailored skirt that reached just below her knees and a white frilly blouse that was appropriate to make such an important announcement. She was soon off to work.

Susan had gone to school and Sumbo was cleaning the living room. Toscin was in the communal kitchen making Ade Bantan's breakfast. Enitan stood up for have a bath and get ready for work. The sun had started to indicate it would be another blistering day. It would be another day for Ade Bantan to spend hours sweating and contemplating the sullen power of the inertia that had become a permanent feature in his life. He often wondered how Enitan's sisters tolerated his certainly corrupting inertia. He could only ascribe almost superhuman levels of tolerance to Enitan, who obviously regarded him as a decent catch. He ought to be chucked out into the streets on his arse, but that hadn't happened and he doubted it ever would. For breakfast, he was served eggs and a few slices of bread. It was unusually simple fare, probably because Toscin and not Sumbo had made the kitchen hers that morning. Sumbo had an inexplicable gift of knowing what he would feel like eating. It wasn't telepathy, just a gift of knowing.

Ade Bantan finished his breakfast and remained on the couch wearing only his khaki shorts. He had began to perspire as he thought about how he was going to endure the vast stretches of minutes he was condemned to observe tick. Enitan went into the bedroom to fetch her vials of moisturizer and her make-up kit and sat on the floor of the living room because she knew he liked to admire her as she prepared herself.

So what are doing today darling?

Oh I'll be working on some ideas for some paintings.

Great I can't wait for when you'll start painting.

Yeah it takes time. Great artists like Picasso and Pollack would leave unfinished work lying around to achieve greater maturity and intensity. I don't want to produce half-arsed work.

I understand baby, but just know that I want to get married this year and have our honeymoon in Europe . . . in Germany and Switzerland, so you have to pace yourself well to ensure all goes according to plan.

I'm doing my best.

See Hankpkaun my friend will be getting married in two months, and I'll be the only left who is single. I don't want that at all and I am doing all I can to avoid that kind of fate.

We'll get there darling… I assure you.

When Enitan was ready, Ade Bantan escorted her to the bus stop where she always took public transport.

I am sick and tired of taking buses to work every bloody day. I must buy a car like all my colleagues are doing. Whaddaya think?

I think that's cool. When do you intend to buy it?

Very soon. In fact, as soon as possible. I'll talk to Papa Osaze tonight when I get back from work. You know he buys second-hand cars for people from across the border. I hear he has excellent contacts with immigration officials, and that's why he is able to do that as a side line.

Great.

Yeah, and we won't have to go around town jumping on and off those filthy rickety buses that are nothing more than deathtraps.

I couldn't agree with you more.

Enitan found a bus and Ade Bantan returned to the apartment through the usual maze of motorcyclists, food vendors, wandering school kids, and cracked roads. It would be another long wait before Enitan came back from work. There was no electricity, so he lay on the couch fanning himself, hoping to come by a coolness he knew wasn't feasible at that time of the day. He wasn't in the mood for conversation with Chidi, who merely offered extended monologues and street-corner gossip. But he also felt oppressed by a growing sense of mental isolation. If he was only able to break out of his embarrassing state of inertia, things would be much better. Sumbo left for work and Toscin also left for the place where she'd found a part-time job. He was left to look down the long empty tunnel of a blazing day.

At about three o'clock in the afternoon, he heard noises rising from the staircase. He flung a shirt over his shoulder and went to see what happening. Chidi had caught Ozase having sex with his nine-year-old sister beneath the staircase. He had immediately raised an alarm and gave the boy a couple of resounding slaps. Osaze was crying when his mother, Mama Osaze, arrived at the scene. She gave him a couple more slaps and told him to go to their apartment to await further punishment. She then turned to Chidi and asked:

What happened?

I saw him fucking his little sister underneath the staircase.

Who could have taught him such a thing?

Kids of today are very fast and sharp. They learn from their friends at school and from watching movies.

The world is coming to an end. I will teach the both of them a lesson they would never forget.

Please take it easy with them, they're only kids and don't know exactly what they're doing.

No. I will not allow evil things in my family. I come from a religious family and will do everything I can to see that we live right. I will stamp this serpent dead in my family. I won't tolerate it.

Mama Osaze went into her apartment and locked the door. She took off her top leaving only her bra. Osaze started to tremble with fear in the corner of the living room near the door. His sister, Angel was in the opposite corner looking far more composed. Mama Osaze fetched a strong but flexible cane—cut from *dogonyaro*—from above the curtain rail. Above the curtains, a cheap, gaudy, large painting of the Christ hung watching the proceedings.

So what were you doing with your sister underneath the staircase?

Nothing mama.

Nothing? So you want to start having babies with your own sister? You are now a full grown man and you want to chase us out of the house so you can be your own boss?

No mama.

Mama Osaze knocked her first son off his feet with a series of blows to the head. He started screaming for his life:

Please mummy, forgive me, I will not do so again. Please mama don't kill me, I will be a good boy from now on. Please mama, let me alone. I beg you, don't kill, help, help, help help, help, I am dying, I am dying, I am dying, please mama don't kill me, I am dying! Forgive me mama, dear father, help me, I don't want to die!

Mama Osaze continued to pummel him with her fists and switched to using the cane when her arms hurt. Osaze continued to scream at the top of his lungs, begging for forgiveness and to be left alone. He bawled until his voice cracked and was reduced to a low growl that sounded as if it was from a traumatized little dog. His mother was panting heavily and spittle dribbled out of the corners of a mouth distorted by rage. Her wrap kept falling off her waist displaying a black see-through underskirt. Angel had started crying too because she knew her fate would be similar. Neighborhoods were banging on the door to the apartment and yelling that Mama Osaze leave her kids alone. She paid them no attention. She stomped on Osaze a few more times and left him too weak to cry any more.

Take off your panties now, she said to Angel.

Angel did as she had been instructed and started trembling. Mama Osaze went into her bedroom and straight to the cupboard where she kept spices and condiments. She grabbed a plastic container that had red hot chili pepper and stormed back into the living room. Angel's weeping had become much louder as the knocking of the neighbors continued.

Stand over here.

Please mummy. I won't do it again.

Shut up and stand over here.

Mama Osaze rubbed some red hot chili into her daughter's crotch and the girl started to scream as if her entire body were itself a yodel floating out of an elongated nightmare.

Mummy! Mummy! Mummy! Mummy! Mummy! Mummy! Mummy! Mummy!

The knocking grew even more furious and still Mama Osaze paid it no heed. Angel rolled on the floor and tore off a t-shirt several sizes smaller than her in agony. She was grabbing hold of the legs of tables and stools as if she was having a seizure. Her mother stood by watching the devastating effects of her medicine. The girl yelled, thrusting her face into the carpet and wetting it with tears and spittle. Blessing, who had been asleep in bedroom, had long since awakened and was also wailing loudly. The knocking continued. Chidi's mother was pleading for Mama Osaze to open the door. Osaze's moaning had fallen a few more registers as he lay on the floor near the door. The neighbors could not quite guess what Mama Osaze was doing to her children. It appeared as if she was trying to drown them in dirty dish water or perhaps she was torturing them with a hot iron searing through their flesh.

Mama Osaze please don't hurt your children. They've had enough. Please, please, please! Amber is here crying her eyes out. She has even fainted. Please Mama Osaze we beg of you, let us in. Don't let the devil gain the upper hand in this fight. Let us settle this matter like responsible adults. Children will always be children and we must do our part in trying to understand their world. Please Mama Osaze forgive the children. They are only children, you must also understand that they do not belong to you alone but to the spirit of the universe. Please Mama Osaze open the door and let us in. You've punished the children enough. Please let us in before something very unfortunate happens. Anger is the twin sister of madness. Please do not let anger into your life. It is something we all regret when we do.

Eventually, Mama Osaze allowed Amber to enter the apartment along with Chidi, his mother, Ade Bantan, and a footballer who lived down the corridor. Angel was on the floor salivating and grasping for breath. Her eyeballs were rolling backwards into her skull. Osaze hadn't caught his breath yet and was still whimpering on the floor. Chidi's mother dashed to Angel who seemed in need of urgent attention.

What did you do to her? asked Chidi's mother as she lifted Angel from the floor with her muscular arms.

Angel pointed at her crotch crying.

Water! Pepper! Water! Pepper! Water! Pepper!

Chidi's mother rushed her to one of the available bathrooms and immediately ran some cold water into a bucket. Angel did not wait for the bucket to fill up before she started trying to throw handfuls of water at her inflamed crotch. Chidi's mother threw more water on her crotch. But Angel kept crying and it was obvious she needed something more inventive to ease her great discomfort. She yelled at Chidi to bring a jar of Vaseline from her apartment. Greasy ointments were thought to ease discomfort caused by burns and other kinds of inflammation; she did not know that grease makes burns much worse. Minutes later, Chidi rushed back bearing some Vaseline. Chidi's mother rubbed a thick slab of grease across the wailing girl's crotch. It seemed to increase her pain so she doused her with more water. Onlookers watched as Chidi's mother grew frantic with trying to ease Angel's agony. Chidi began to complain:

What kind of woman is this? How can she rub pepper into a little girl's privates? This is sheer madness and unadulterated evil. Pure evil. Does she want to kill her? If I had known this is what she would do, I wouldn't have told her. I mean, we all did the same when we were kids, so what is all this bullshit hypocrisy as if she never had it up her own arse as a kid. This is total bullshit. I regret this day. I have never seen such a thing in my life. That woman is deranged. Honestly, I regret this day because I made a great mistake. This is something we could have all joked about after a couple of slaps. Instead, the bloody witch tries to kill her own children.

Angel's wailing continued, punctuated by sudden, disconcerting screams. Mama Osaze remained in her apartment while her neighbors tried to allay her daughter's discomfort.

How are we going to solve this problem? I've done everything I can to make the pain go away. It seems the water and Vaseline solution is not working. I don't know what else to do.

After about an hour, Angel was taken into Chidi's apartment to lie down. No position satisfied her. She couldn't lie with her legs together, she couldn't lie on her stomach, and although she had barely eaten all day, she couldn't eat anything. She kept whimpering and Chidi's mother started to fear that her temperature might shoot up. Neighbors kept showing up at the door of the apartment to offer their sympathies. She couldn't respond and seemed not to recognize where she was. After a while, she asked for a drink of water, which Chidi fetched for her. She remained on the floor crying and whimpering until sundown when her father returned from work. Papa Osaze carried her to his apartment with a barely a word of gratitude to Chidi's mother who had done all within her means to pacify the child. Mama Osaze remained in her apartment and didn't come out.

Ade Bantan was displeased with what had happened. He felt saddened that Chidi had reported what he saw to Mama Osaze. Anytime he imagined the pain the girl was going through, chills coursed through his body. He knew he had to keep his distance from Mama Osaze. A woman who would go to the extent she did was capable of anything. He couldn't wait for Enitan to return from work to tell her what had transpired. Everyone in the yard seemed saddened. When

Enitan returned, Sumbo and Toscin told her about Angel's ordeal in whispers.

Enitan was aghast, but she hid it. She had a matter to discuss with Papa Osaze and didn't want to adopt a mood that would prevent her from saying what she had in mind. During the day, she had made a large cash withdrawal as deposit for a car she wanted Papa Osaze to buy for her across the border. She called Sumbo and Toscin to the living room. She told them she had part of the money for a car she had been waiting to buy through the assistance of Papa Osaze. She wanted them together with Ade Bantan to be there when she handed over the cash.

Enitan asked them all to give her a few minutes while she changed into something more comfortable. She emerged from the bedroom in a brownish nylon gown that had snakelike patterns. It was comfortable—sleeveless and loose fitting. The four of them went next door and knocked. Usually Osaze made it his chore to answer the door, but he was still too distraught to carry out the function. Papa Osaze opened the door.

Yes my sister, what is it?

Thank you Papa Osaze. How was your day? I hope it went well.

It went very well thank you. Would like to come inside?

No. It is very hot. We can all go to the balcony where there is more fresh air to talk.

Very well then. Let me just put on a shirt.

Papa Osaze dashed in and returned with an unbuttoned shirt across his shoulders.

Thanks you for making time for us Papa Osaze this evening. You may recall my telling you that I would be coming to talk with you about something important soon. You are looked upon as one of the role models in our compound.

Thank you.

No, really. You are hardworking, honest, and you are a very spiritual person. You have a good family and have been blessed in so many ways. It is good to admit when something is good. It is right for us to point out excellent qualities in others, which we can also use as yardsticks to improve ourselves. We all want to make progress in our lives and escape from the clutches of poverty. Is this not so? Well I for one like the good things of life. I will come to the point. I know that you sometimes buy second-hand cars for people across the border, and I would like you to serve as my agent for the purchase of a car. In short, I want to give you money to buy a car for me.

So what type of car do you want?

Something feminine. A Japanese car preferably, with two doors. I like metallic grey, metallic blue, or black.

Black? Exclaimed Sumbo. Why black?

It is not bad. But I only want it as a last resort. Use your imagination, don't always follow the crowd. Anyway, Papa

Osaze, to return to our matter . . . I want a solid car, one that would be able to withstand the potholes and rigors of this damned city.

I know what you mean my sister.

Thank you Papa Osaze. I have half of the money you told me it would cost and I will pay the other half once the car is delivered. How long did you say that it would take to deliver it again?

About a week or so all things considered.

I will really appreciate it if you can help me in this matter. I really want to take my baby cruising around town, she said, giving Ade Bantan a hug.

There will be no problem . . . I have been doing this job for a few years now and I know all the right routes and right immigration officers.

I trust you Papa Osaze; that is why I have come to you. I could have gone to any one of my brothers, and, in fact, my cousin, Ulmanmadu, sometimes does this kind of business. But I wanted to use someone who would tell me no stories about things going wrong. I want someone who really knows the borders and the customs people and who will deliver on time. I am aware that some so-called agents take something like three months to deliver. I don't need the unnecessary heartache of waiting for something I paid for after having sweated a big part of my life for the money. I don't need that kind of rubbish. I want to live long and I don't want to have a heart attack at such a young age. So that is why I am giving up this money for you to buy a car for me.

Papa Osaze received the money which was tied into two large wads with rubber bands.

I have heard you my sister, and I appreciate it very much for putting your trust in me. You all know me well in this yard. I am spiritual man, a man of strong principle, and I have never duped anyone in my life. That is not part of my destiny. I was brought up well by my parents and that is also how I am bringing up all of my children. We believe in doing good and making a difference in all that we do. So, my sister, let us cut a long story short. On the promised day, about a week from today, your car will arrive. I don't want to talk too much because action speaks louder than words. As much as I am a peaceful man, as you all know, I am also a man of action. I believe in action so that we can change our lives and the world. I will leave the rest of the talking until I have delivered your car.

Thank you Papa Osaze for taking on this job. I really appreciate it.

Thank you my sister.

Good night.

Enitan, Ade Bantan, Sumbo, and Toscin returned to their apartment. Susan was already fast asleep on the floor. Her mouth was slightly open, but she wasn't drooling. Enitan reminded her sisters again to start sleeping in the living room. It appeared Susan had got the message. Ade Bantan returned to his usual position on the couch to wait for Sumbo and Toscin to change into night clothes in the bedroom. The door of the apartment leading to the main corridor was open as it usually was. Ade Bantan was puzzled that Enitan didn't bother to lock the door which could be easily be shatttered by a good kick from a hard-boned miscreant.

Many families in the yard also left the doors open despite the large number of vagrants, thugs, and thieves in the neighborhood. It was believed the robbers would not carry out operations in the area where they lived. It was to close to home, too close to the bone. But Ade Bantan didn't believe such thug rationality could be applied in all seasons and under all conditions. If you gave a thief half a chance, there was a very strong possibility he would want to try his luck just one more time. And what if some of the thugs were kleptomaniacs or serial rapists? What if they were victims of some twisted nature or sheer illogic? What if they were compelled to act without self-control? Such gnarled natures were frequently seen among criminal elements.

Ade Bantan believed it was better to take cautionary measures when necessary and possible as opposed to being a victim of some horrific ordeal that would irrevocably change one's life. Enitan didn't seem to care. He saw her stance as a mix of naiveté and streetwise foolhardiness. He often wondered whether, if they were to be victims of an armed robbery attack, he would be the first to receive the stick for the simple reason that he was the only male in the apartment.

Sumbo eventually came out with a wrap around her breasts. She hadn't taken off her bra, making Ade wonder how she was going to sleep in such unbearable heat. The electricity had not been cut, but the ceiling fan made no difference as it merely circulated waves of heat. Toscin came out with her own wrap around smaller breasts.

Let's go sleep inside darling it's getting late.

Enitan pulled the unmoving Ade Bantan from the couch. He yawned and put on his slippers. He was keen to spend the night in the bedroom after so many nights on the couch but he didn't want to appear too eager to deprive the girls of the pleasure on sleeping in the bedroom. Sleeping in the bedroom also had its own drawbacks. It was hotter because the only window was smaller and air had much less space to circulate in the knotted barrage of odds and ends and stuff.

In spite of the intense heat, Ade Bantan was still willing to provide Enitan some of the best care he could. Enitan had nothing on apart from a blue g-string with faint grey stripes. Her underwear accented her fine figure. It immediately brought his cock to attention.

Come on baby, let me give you a massage after a hard day's work.

Oh you're such a darling.

What am I here for if not to give you pleasure?

Hmm. Please start on my left shoulder, it hurts.

Ade Bantan stooped by Enitan's side on the mattress and began to work on her body. He started slowly and became gradually vigorous as he softened her skin with his strong arms. The softeness of her skin served to maintain his

155

hardness and he feared he might ejaculate before they had had sex. He tried to let his mind wander off into other zones. He tried focusing on the benefits of tantric sex, marathon sex sessions by people who subscribed to transcendental meditation and the dissolution of the ego. For a moment, he managed to trick his conscious mind, but he couldn't maintain the discipline as the softness of Enitan's skin called him back to earth. As he was about to enter her she said:

Use a condom.

Ade Bantan had a packet in one of the side pockets of his traveling bag, which he was able to locate after a bit of rummaging. He tore up the wrapper and tried to slip on the condom, but in his clumsiness, he ripped it. He brought out another, and this time managed to put it on successfully. Enitan, who had been aroused by his kisses and caresses, was ready for him. She signaled him to switch off the light, as it was possible for those in the living room to see them making love. But he ignored her because he wanted to enjoy the sight of her skin tone. He kept trying to think of matters unrelated to sex so that he could prolong their pleasure. He eventually ejaculated and rolled off her. After a few minutes used catching his breath, he removed the used condom and threw it on the floor. Enitan told him to switch off the light which he did. They both fell asleep.

The following morning, Toscin woke them up by switching on the light. She wanted to get ready for a job interview and had to get dressed. She got a little piece of soap and her toothbrush in the bowl where they were kept. Covering herself with a sheet, she removed her shorts and t-shirt in preparation for going to the bathroom. Toscin must

156

have seen the used condoms on the floor where Ade Bantan had flung them, but she pretended to be unaware of them. Enitan hadn't quite fully awakened; she tried to catch some more sleep in spite of the brightness of the light on her sleepy eyes. Ade Bantan wasn't ready to wake up yet either, and turned his face down in an attempt to dim some of the glare of the light bulb. Toscin did not dress in the bedroom, but took a tube of body lotion together with her clothes to the living room.

After Toscin had had her bath, Sumbo woke Susan up to prepare for school. Susan stripped naked while Ade Bantan watched with half-closed eyes as she fetched some soap and a toothbrush. She apparently didn't see the used condoms on the floor. In less than ten minuntes, she was back from her bath and quickly applied the lotion on her self while she assumed a stooped position. He continued to watch while Enitan slept. Sumbo came into the bedroom to see how Susan was doing, chiding her not to be late for school. By then, she had noticed the used condoms, but ignored them. He shut his eyes tightly to be sure that it would appear that he was still asleep. A short while after Toscin left the apartment to attend her interview, Susan left for school. Sumbo began her daily chore of cleaning up the living room. All the yard was abuzz with the boisterous voices of children getting set for school. There was the din of aluminum utensils dropping in the corridor and in the kitchens. Vehicles were hooting loudly on the streets and food vendors had started making vociferous calls to the customers.

Ade Bantan could sleep no longer, but he lay on the mattress since he had to reason to get up. The noises eventually got to Enitan and she was forced to wake up. She stretched out her arms kneeling on the mattress and yawned. She then sat with her back against wall.

Hi darling did you sleep well?

Yes thank you. And how are you this morning? What are your plans for today?

Oh the usual . . . what would I be doing apart from work?

Busy woman. Well, we all know you're doing it for a good cause.

Let's hope so. What would you like for breakfast this morning so I can leave instructions with Sumbo?

It is still too early to say. I have to let my taste buds wake up, and they awaken much more slowly than the rest of my body.

Interesting. Wait a minute . . . what are those on the floor over there.

Fuck.

Oh my god. You left those damn condoms on the floor since last night and all my sisters would have seen them. What sort of crap is this?

I don't think they saw them.

What do you mean you don't think they saw them? Of course they saw them, but being the well-bred girls that they are they would pretend not to. How could you be so careless? I didn't believe you could ever do such a thing.

I'm sorry.

No. this is absolutely inexcusable. This is most embarrassing. What would my sisters think of me? That all they do is fuck, that is it, they do nothing but fuck and they have the audacity to leave dirty condoms lying everywhere.

Your sisters haven't done or said anything to indicate they saw the condoms.

I've told you that they won't but can you read what's in their minds? They will keep it to themselves and that is the worst part.

I am sorry.

Better be and please don't ever let it happen again.

Enitan snatched the used condoms and wrappers from the floor and got ready to go to the bathroom. As she did, she kept hissing and cursing. Ade Bantan knew better than to antagonize her more by answering back. It was better to ignore her until her ire had subsided. While she was in the bath, he started to think of ways to please her before she left for work. What joke could he tell that would make her laugh? He strained his brain, but couldn't come up with any. He had to find something to allay her annoyance as he didn't want her to venture to work in such an awful mood. Then it struck him that the hair in her armpits had become unseemly. Her pubic hair also needed to be shaved. That was what he would do, he would shave off her body hair. He went to his traveling bag and brought out a fresh disposable razor. He then lay on the mattress and waited for her to complete her bath. A few minutes later she returned.

I hope you have cooled down now. I don't want you to go to work in that mood.

Then you should stop doing things that would annoy me.

I've said I am sorry darling. Hey darling the hairs in your armpits are showing.

That can't be true. I shaved last week.

Seriously, I can see it from here and you know you like wearing sleeveless tops. A woman of your standing shouldn't be caught dead with hair in her armpits. Can I shave them for you?

Please do, but hurry up, I don't want to be late.

Ok lie on the mattress my goddess so that I can prepare you for the shrine.

Ade Bantan carefully removed the wisps of hair from Enitan's armpits and pointed out that her pubic hair needed shaving too. He fetched a pair of scissors from the window ledge. He declined using a razor because he didn't want her to develop a rash. That turned out to be an error. Enitan was lying naked on the mattress as he shaved her. He asked her to spread her legs so he could reach hidden spots that needed snipping. But he was distracted by the sight of her labia. The

160

folds of her vulva never ceased to amaze him. They were full of richness, mystery, character, and variety. In his distraction, he cut her slightly on the spot that had most strongly attracted him. Enitan let out a scream.

What have you done? You cut me! Shit!

I'm so sorry.

You're always sorry.

I really mean it Enitan. Please forgive me. Let me see if it is bad.

All I know it that it hurts.

Ade Bantan stooped over her crotch to see what damage he had done. It wasn't much. He made out a line of blood less than half an inch long. He knew she would feel awful for the next few days any time she took a leak. He had worsened the situation that he had hoped to repair. He knew it wasn't wise to offer to see her to the bus stop as he did on most days. To do so, would be to expose himself to her relentless sulking and muted curses. As usual, he would begin his day by marking time on the couch.

Thirty minutes after Enitan left for work, Sumbo also went out, and Ade Bantan was left alone in the apartment. There was a power cut and the sun began its dominance. The minutes ticked by very slowly. Ade Bantan could not form a connection between the desultory visual images in his head and the actual physical effort needed to realize them. He felt sickened by his inertia but had no idea of how to go about confronting his chronic listlessness. He felt oppressed by apathy and the daunting omnipresence of time. Time dishes out doses of itself like juice squeezed from bitter herbs. Each passing minute was a drop of bitter liquid. There seemed to be a conspiracy between the blistering sun and the infinity of time. His infinitesimal head lay jammed in between as blood from his soul was slowly drained away. In spite of the heat, he managed to sleep. This was probably because he hadn't been sleeping well. Sweat poured out of his face, neck and lithe torso.

Ade Bantan must have been asleep for about an hour when he was awakened by the noises of children in the yard. Chidi ran into the apartment and urged to come and watch a free fight.

Free fight?

Yes! Zakari is having a street fight with Buddy Joe! Come quick!

Ade Bantan got up without bothering to put on his shirt, which was lying on an arm-rest. He also didn't bother to put on his slippers as he went after Chidi to the balcony at the end of the corridor. Below on the street, Zakari, a security guard who worked at one of the houses on the street was squaring off with Buddy Joe, an expert at judo and tai chi. Zakari was about six four and Buddy Joe was a mere five eight. The disparity in height was glaring. Zakari's normal demeanor was rather quiet, so it was rather surprising to see him engaging in a street fight in broad daylight. Both men had taken off their shirts revealing well-formed torsos. Zakari who was rumored to have descended from Fulani stock had muscles that appeared carved from steel. His movements weren't subtle and fluid but his strength lay in his near physical impenetrability.

Buddy Joe on the other hand, moved like a sack of melons on a fast-flowing stream. His muscles were not at all hard like Zakari's, but were slithery and flexible. He also had considerable patience in facing his opponent, whose anger was clearly demonstrated in his tactical maneuvers. Zakari seemed like a raging wildebeest about to crush a prey. Buddy Joe executed feints and smiled as if the entire fight were a joke. But it was no joke; he was only employing his considerable skill and cunning to throw Zakari off balance and then take him unawares. Suddenly, Buddy Joe, using his lack of height, ducked underneath the imposing Zakari, sweeping him off his feet. Zakari was hurled onto Buddy Joe's shoulders and thrown onto hot asphalt. It was a devastating throw.

Ade Bantan felt his teeth grate and shivers course through his body. He felt great sympathy for Zakari. But Zakari wasn't through yet. When Buddy Joe started to pummel him on the asphalt, Zakari grabbed him and pulled him into a wrestling hold that brought the fight to a stalemate. The kids who lived on the streets kept cheering the brawlers and extolling them to continue fighting. Zakari, who was beneath Buddy Joe on the ground, was not about to let go because that would most certainly expose him to the latter's blows after he had secured an advantage. And so, Zakari maintained his hold in order to weaken Buddy Joe.

Just then, one of Zakari's cronies emerged through the crowd of spectators and dealt Buddy Joe a flurry of powerful kicks to his ribs. Zakari released his hold and allowed Buddy Joe to withdraw. Buddy Joe fetched his shirt where it lay at the mouth of a sewer and brushed of grains of sand from his back and torso. He started to boast that he would have destroyed Zakari had his friend not intervened. Zakari walked back to his shed with a gait that was a cross between a limp and a swagger. He was too proud to display his pain at being thrown over with such devastating force. He would have to spend weeks nursing his wounds in the stark silence of his bare guard post. Once he had healed, he would have to teach that interloper a lesson.

Buddy Joe had come to the neighborhood claiming to be an expert in every known martial art and that he could take on any guy in the area and give him the beating of his life. He showed no one any respect and bragged about his popularity with the kids and girls. He said he wanted to be addressed as mayor on account of his popularity. He had even started making money by teaching kids in the area some judo; this made him even more arrogant. Older neighborhood lads felt that it was time to put him in his proper place. It was time to dish him a good combination of blows and kicks to shut him up for good. Zakari had wanted the honor of shutting up the boastful Buddy Joe for good and had been disappointed to have been thwarted. He had to go back to the drawing-board and devise a new strategy for conquest.

On the streets, the kids kept chatting excitedly about the fight. Some of them ran behind Buddy Joe telling him they wanted to join his judo and tai chi classes. They told him he was their hero and they wanted to be like him. Their mothers stood on their porches, shaking their heads in disbelief and confusion. There were no role models for their kids except gangsters and street thugs.

Ade Bantan went back into the apartment and returned to the couch. It felt a trifle cooler to escape the direct heat of the sun. The wall beside him was hot. Everywhere was steaming hot and the minutes ticked slowly. He was disgusted at the turn his life was taking. He was been reduced to being a spectator of cheap street brawls. The fight had been a non-starter from a visual point of view. It had no aesthetic merit whatsoever. It was now impossible to sleep after his brain had been fired by the excitement caused by the fight.

Mama Osaze was furious that people were leaving the toilets unflushed and was bemoaning the fact on the corridor. It was difficult to conceive what she had in mind about hygiene as there were only six toilets in the entire yard. Occupants brought in guests and family on a daily basis, so all the toilets and baths were constantly in use. Families took turns at doing the cleaning, but mere daily cleaning, usually in the morning, was not enough to keep the toilets and baths in a decent state because just too many people had to use them everyday.

Oftentimes, the water system would break down and toilets and bathrooms had to be left uncleaned until the water supply was restored. During such periods, the entire compound reeked. Ade Bantan would find excuses to go on long walks and pass the time smoking cigarettes. It was enough agony dealing with the insufferable heat and ennui. But once the water supply broke down, he had to add the stench of excreta to his burden of worries. Mama Osaze had cause to complain, but could not produce the sort of thinking that would rectify the problem. Most of the occupants of the yard usually went out to work and didn't return until nightfall. On weekends, many had private social engagements to attend and many went to church services. Everyone seemed to be so engrossed in the own little worlds that they could not find the time to come together for a solution. Mama Osaze didn't take all this into account in her frequent rants about hygiene in the yard. Somehow, she thought her rants would will a permanent solution to the problem into existence.

A few minutes later, Waddadah, a friend of Enitan, walked in and said hello. Ade Bantan told her that Enitan wasn't back from work yet, and Waddadah said she would wait. She was dressed in blue jeans and a red body-hugging t-shirt. She didn't talk much and seemed to be a bit aggrieved. Ade Bantan felt it wasn't his place to ask if anything was wrong. He knew that in time, everything would be revealed to him.

Waddadah went into the bedroom and scooped up a stack of old magazines, which she brought into the living room and started browsing on the floor. Ade Bantan could sense she didn't talk much and felt it was better to let her be. He reached for a magazine and tried to fan himself from time to time. Still the minutes ticked by at a snail's pace and the heat bore into the flesh. A terrible combination. Waddadah continued to go through the stack of magazines while Ade Bantan fanned himself intermittently with a soggy old pamphlet.

The heat of the sun gradually decreased as dusk approached. Ade Bantan's spirit rose with the imminence of sundown. It meant Enitan would return soon and when she did, the pace of everything would pick up. There would always be something to say, laugh about, or cause some provocation. Susan returned from school, saluted Ade Bantan and Waddadah, rushed into the bedroom, took off her uniform, scrambled into her home clothes, and then dashed into the courtyard behind the building to play with kids in the yard.

Toscin came in and exclaimed on seeing Waddadah.

Wonders shall never end! Hello stranger! Good to see you! Long time.

Good to see you too.

How are you?

I'm fine.

It's been such a long time! Where have you been?

Oh doing stuff here and there.

You look great.

Thank you, you're not looking bad yourself.

So what's been happening to you? Are you now married?

No, you know I can't possibly be married with you knowing about it.

Well that's true. I was wondering what could have happened to you. Have you had something to eat?

No.

Why is that? There is so much stuff at home. We've got yam, potatoes, rice, and vegetable soup. What would you like to have?

I'm not yet hungry and I think I'll wait for Enitan to return from work.

All right. Suit yourself. It's great to see you again. Have you met Ade Bantan, my sister's fiancée? He's been very kind.

Uncle, I trust you've met our very good friend, Waddadah. I won't call her my sister's very good friend because he belongs to all of us. Please introduce yourself.

I am Waddadah.

I am Ade Bantan.

Nice to meet you.

Nice to meet you, too.

Uncle, is Susan back from school yet?

Yes.

But where is she?

I suppose she's out in the courtyard playing with other kids.

Has she done her school homework yet?

I don't think so.

That girl needs a good spanking. She's below average at school and my sister spends a lot of money for her tuition. What annoys me is that she plays with kids much younger than she is. You need to see her in their midst holding court like an old mama.

Oh give the poor girl a break.

No this is a serious issue. All she does is play about. It really pisses me off.

She'll get over it. And how did your interview go?

Not too bad, I hope. The only snag is that they asked for the original copies of my certificates and I had to tell them I hadn't completed my university course.

How did you get invited to the interview in the first place?

I met one of the top guys on the interview panel and I think he pulled some strings to get me invited.

And what is he getting for such a big favor?

Nothing. He seems to be a good guy.

Do you think you stand a chance of getting the job?

It's hard to say. There were fifty thousand applicants for ten job spaces.

Whoah! that is a pretty tough situation.

Yeah but you have to have faith. You have to take the bull by the horns and confront your destiny. That is the least you can do.

I wish you good luck with it.

Thanks. I need it. I've got to change into something more comfortable. Please give me a minute.

So what do you do for a living Waddadah?

I work at a radio station.

What do you do there?

I'm an announcer.

Do you like it?

It's not bad. I get to meet important people.

That's good.

I suppose I can't complain. And you what do you do for a living.

I'm a painter.

What exactly do you do? Paint houses?

No I do portraits. I'm an artist.

Do you make any money from it?

Sometimes.

It's is difficult to make a living here as an artist.

It is tough everywhere being an artist.

So why do you do it?

I suppose for the love of it.

Love, is there such a thing nowadays?

I suppose I'm an old fashioned romantic.

As they say, different strokes . . .

For different folks.

Thank you. I wish you best of luck with what you do.

Thank you. I need it.

Toscin emerged from the bedroom in a red mini-skirt and a skimpy sky blue top.

Uncle, are you ready to eat now?

No, I'll wait for Enitan to come back from work before I eat.

It seems everyone is waiting for my sister to return before they eat. I guess I'm the odd one out because I'm starving and I'm going to have myself something to eat.

Great enjoy yourself big girl.

The final rays of the sun had disappeared, and then, to everyone's surprise, the electricity was restored. Toscin didn't have to go to the kitchen with a kerosene lamp. The kitchen, which was used by eight families, had charcoal black tables and cupboards in every corner. The floor was black with soot, as were the walls, which had been painted dark blue. A single exposed bulb hung from the ceiling providing the only source of light. The light was weak and the corners of the kitchen remained largely unlit, thereby providing a place of refuge for cockroaches and rats. The kitchen had space for a window that had lost all of its glass, and so sunlight and rain gained easy entry.

Toscin opened Enitan's wooden cupboard and brought out a grease-smeared pot of vegetable soup. She also brought out a kerosene stove on which she heated some water to make at least three bowls of *amala*. She yelled out to Susan to come for her food. Minutes later, Susan emerged from the courtyard below and collected a slap on the face for not doing her homework before she was granted her bowl of food. Susan's formerly happy disposition evaporated and she covered her face with the crook of her arm and headed for the apartment. Ade Bantan could see that Susan had been reprimanded but didn't bother to ask what for, because he knew Toscin had been angry with her. Waddadah hardly looked up from the stack of magazines that lay between her feet.

Good evening.

How are you doing Susan?

Fine thank you.

Good; enjoy your meal.

It was dark now and Enitan hadn't returned. Ade Bantan wondered what was keeping her. He hated to be in a state of perpetual waiting. It made him think about all sorts of unsavory things. Where the hell was she? Was she with someone else? Was she spending some louche downtime with her boss with him trying to get into her pants again? Was she out enjoying herself with some of her colleagues at a bar somewhere? Had she been invited to some private house for a round of drinks to mark the end of the workday? He was getting overwhelmed with having to dwell on such thoughts almost everyday.

Before he ran out of creative juices, he had sometimes romantic fantasies about being a stay-at-home partner. He had had dreams of filling up canvases with stunning visual images at home while his partner toiled at more practical issues like bring food home. His partner was to support him until he had become financial strong enough to take care of both of them. This was his initial dream before he got waylaid on the couch. He could still pinpoint all the factors that had created his seemingly insurmountable creative lethargy. He was sometimes disgusted with himself for not telling Enitan the truth about his situation. She would probably suggest he attend the white garment church down the street. He wouldn't want to add that manner of solution to his lengthening litany of worries. It was enough that he had to somehow find the strength to pull himself out of his creative cul-de-sac.

And now, the corrosive chancre of jealousy had started to slowly gnaw at his entrails. It wasn't a pleasant feeling at all. Under better conditions, it was unworthy of him. It was unworthy of any man who had the good fortune to be a stay-at-home partner. Enitan had given him a resource that had an inestimable value: time. As an artist, it was a resource that he

173

couldn't get enough of, and which, had he been in a better frame of mind, he could employ as a launch pad to take a leap toward the inscrutable and mystical pinacle of greatness. But his mind, rather his spirit, had decided to go to sleep on him. Riches that could have strayed into his life were sauntering past him at an alarming rate, while the seconds wasted annoyingly tickled his nostrils as he sweated his arse off lying on the couch. These kind of thoughts he could discuss with no one. Not Enitan, Sumbo, Toscin, Joshua, or Chidi. These were matters that had to live and die within him.

Enitan came entered the apartment and screamed when she saw Waddadah.

Look who is here! Waddadah! Where did you drop from? Darling, this is one of my dearest friends who abandoned me for such a long time.

I didn't abandon you my dear; I've been having serious problems.

What kind of problems? Work-related problems or relationship problems?

We need to sit down and talk. It isn't something I can finish telling you in a matter of minutes.

Do you want us to go into the bedroom and talk then?

That would be nice.

Ok let go. Excuse us darling.

See you later ladies.

Enitan and Waddadah entered the bedroom and made themselves comfortable on the mattress. Waddadah then burst into tears.

What's wrong my darling?

I don't know where to start.

Start anywhere and just let out whatever toxins you've been keeping within you. You look so sad.

It's bad, so bad.

What is bad?

I got into this terrible relationship with this guy and it has turned out to be the greatest mistake of my life.

You have a man in your life?

Yes. I have been with this arsehole of a guy for almost two years now. He's just trying to take over my entire life. It all started off well and he seemed nice at first.

They usually are in the beginning. What's his name?

Eddie Booh.

Eddie Booh? What a name. Where did you meet such a guy?

It doesn't matter. The point is, I fell in with him and he moved into my crib a year ago. He was between jobs when I met him, but he had some savings, so initially money wasn't a problem. I thought he would spend his savings job hunting, but this guy sat on his arse all day smoking pot in the house. Eventually, he finished off all his savings smoking pot and drinking wine, still without getting a job. I'm so damned tired after spending hours in traffic and poisonous exhaust fumes, yet when I get back from work, he wants to fuck the living daylights out of me. He doesn't make me any dinner and he expects me to cook and then come directly to bed with him.

He's such a bastard.

He's worse than a bastard. And now, I have to put up with his jealousy because he's become so insecure. If I'm late because of traffic jams, he thinks it's because I've been with someone else. This has been the daily routine of my life. I wake up at four o'clock in the morning, drag my arse off to the bus stop, and take the three-hour drive for a day of soul-destroying work. Then I get home, and this man expects me to cook and then fuck him. If I complain that I'm tired, he tells me that I'm a slut and that I've out fucking someone else. Can you imagine? I mean he lives in my flat but he's become so obnoxious that I dread going back to my own crib at the end of the day. I was so tired today and I didn't want to have to go through the usual crap, so that's why I'm here. I hope you can put me up for the night while I do some thinking to get me out of this mess.

No problem. You know you're always welcome.

Thanks my darling.

But I don't know if you would be comfortable here. There are so many of us sleeping here now and sometimes my cousins drop in unannounced to spend the night. But, I tell you what, I have a friend. I think he's gay, but he hasn't confirmed it to me. He would be very happy to put you up for a night or a few days. I think it would be a good idea to check with him and see what we can arrange. How about that?

I'm willing to give it a try.

Enitan asked Ade Bantan to come with them on their visit to Fine Boy Payne's place, about six bus stops away. As they walked to the bus stop, they encountered petty traders on the streets selling stuff like onions, pepper, tomatoes, and homemade liquor with the aid of kerosene lamps. Across the thick canvas of the night, flames of fire blazed with a dazzling mix of tacky brilliance and an air of foreboding. Voices continued to hail passersby hawking their wares. Bars selling liquor had set out chairs and tables by the street. Revelers were guffawing as they quaffed warm bottles of beer because there wasn't any electricity. Commercial motorcyclists were meandering through interminable maps of potholes risking their limbs and those of other street users. Pimps had started to solicit clients for their women. Families were trying to put together whatever scraps of food they could. Babies were wailing from the heat and many other discomforts. Workers returning late were brushing past other pedestrians in total exhaustion. Another day had come and gone with no significant change.

Enitan and her little party found a rickety bus that was going in the direction of Fine Boy Payne's place. It was a boon that the bus was only half full, but it choked riders with clouds of smoke and gave a noisy croak anytime the gears were changed. Enitan and Waddadah continued to chat amid the din. Ade Bantan hardly joined their conversation. Not that he couldn't have if he had wanted to, but the women were discussing matters he didn't really have an opinion about.

There were no streetlights as they headed to Fine Boy Payne's place. It was a mystery how so many motorists avoided death and disaster on unlit streets filled with potholes and impatient pedestrians who kept dashing across the path of speeding vehicles. Beggars and the mentally ill shared the available spaces on the cracked, filthy pavements. Thugs and thieves were loitering in the shadows underneath bridges, readying their guns and cleaning their knives. There was always the blood of a few victims to spill. No big deal, just a way of life.

The bus reached the point where Enitan, Waddadah, and Ade Bantan had to jump off. Fine Boy Payne's neighborhood didn't differ much from Enitan's in terms of character and feel. Children in bare feet were playing soccer on the streets with an orange plastic ball. The ball kept rolling into a sewer filled with muck; each time, one of them would dash after it and scoop it up with their bare hands. They would then shake off some of the slimy water and toss the ball back into play. Their voices rent the air amid the hooting of motorcyclists. Enitan and company passed by dark beer dens, brothels, and old unkempt buildings filled with three or four generations of people. Some streets had gates that reached waist-high, installed to deter armed robbers from gaining entry or escaping after midnight. Tongues of fire from kerosene lamps dotted everywhere. Masses of people crammed into every crevice; in the sewers, rats were emerging soaking wet for a night of work and pilfering; colonies of mosquitoes danced over the edges of gutters. People plagued with malaria and typhoid groaned atop wet bed sheets in damp, crammed rooms. The bitter reek of fever escaped from old buildings and shadowed the congested streets. It was difficult to know who had a sick head and who didn't. The bitter stench of fever touched everything in sight and all that was hidden.

When they reached Fine Boy Payne's street, a party was going on. Grey canopies had been put on the middle of the street for guests. A few drunks were dancing wildly on the streets. Groups of people sat chatting on chairs scattered around. There were empty liquor bottles all over the asphalt. White disposable plates lay on the middle of the street with a few grains of jollof rice, which even the street urchins ignored because they were negligible. Emaciated dogs were licking the grains off the plates and the ground; the revelers were too drunk to notice. It was hard to tell precisely which building was hosting the party because the chairs and canopies covered the length of three derelict buildings. Enitan and company made their way through the canopies, empty bottles, paper plates, plastic, and trash that lay scattered across the street. Fine Boy Payne lived three buildings further down.

When they got to the entranceway of Fine Boy Payne's building, they found his front door standing open. They felt lucky to have found him at home. Loud music was blaring out of his bare living room. Fine Boy Payne's apartment had three bedrooms painted in a dull shade of green. He lived with another bachelor, who was busy fetching drinks. They had a number of guests_lying around the bare living room floor. They were all men and had taken off their shirts because of the intense heat. It was obvious they had all been drinking.

Enitan knew immediately that it wouldn't be possible for Fine Boy Payne to accommodate Waddadah for the night. She didn't even bother to ask him if he could do her the favor. There was no point. So she made it appear that they had come on simple visit. Fine Boy Payne was pleased to see her, as usual. More drinks were produced. Enitan and Waddadah were served some soda while Ade Bantan settled for a beer. Enitan chatted with Fine Boy Payne about work and general issues as the music system blasted out loud R&B sounds. After their drinks, Enitan beckoned Waddadah and Ade Bantan, indicating that it was time to go.

Fine Boy Payne escorted his guests through the trash-filled streets to the bus stop. There was a cacophony of discordant sounds coming from virtually every house. The kids that had been playing soccer were still busy with their games. They made their way gingerly through the maze of noisy children and the dark orifices of gutters before reaching a bus stop choked with masses of waiting commuters. Eventually, they scrambled into a bus that had a couple of vacant seats and waved Fine Boy Payne goodbye. The two women sat on the last available seats while Ade Bantan squeezed himself beside the conductor on a hot metallic ledge behind the driver's seat. After a few minutes, his butt was getting hot and sore. To make matters worse, the conductor stank like dead fish. He felt nauseous. He started to regret having agreed to come along.

Trips on the smoke-filled buses were horrible. The buses themselves were filled with sweaty bodies squeezed into every available corner. Being out in the streets was even worse. The broken pavements were covered in sewer muck. Discordant noises from gloomy looking buildings filled with anger and hate assailed the spirit as one ambled through the craters on the streets. Motorists and motorbikers swore at pedestrians who were only trying to figure out how to make their way through garbage-strewn streets. Street vendors cursed you for not buying their wares. Toothless grandmothers tried to con you into buying rotten food. Wet rats scurried over your feet as you inched your way along. Mosquitoes flew into your ears and nostrils. You cried hallelujah each time a bag of shit hurled from a window missed you and landed on the street just before you. Enitan had made it appear as if they were going on a little pleasure excursion, but to Ade Bantan, it was an arduous trek through the innards of perpetual aggravation.

They were all tired and sweaty when they got back to Enitan's apartment. Sumbo, Toscin, and Susan were still awake. Sumbo got up and went into the kitchen to serve out dinner meant for three. Enitan and Waddadah ate from the same dish while sitting on the floor, while Ade Bantan sat on the couch. He had been starving, but the meal gave him little real satisfaction. Already hot and sweaty from the visit to Fine Boy Payne's apartment, the living room seemed to harbor even more heat because so many of them were crowded in a small room with only one window. The buildings in the neighborhood were built so close to one another that the air had no free circulation. He feared living in such crammed quarters was a sure recipe for tuberculosis, cholera, or meningitis. It was a mystery how there hadn't been a major outbreak of one of the diseases yet. Many already suffered from malaria or typhoid. He wanted to get out of the area before one of them got to him; he could feel them lurking beneath the carpet where he sat. He could sense them festering inside and between the decrepit buildings. He had to do something before they crept up to him and took him away.

After their meals, Enitan and Ade Bantan retired to the bedroom for the night. Wearing the same jeans that she had worn all day, Waddadah slept with Sumbo, Toscin, and Susan in the living room, all sleeping on the floor. Ade Bantan didn't try to make love to Enitan because so many active ears were near. It was the price one had to pay for not being able to afford some privacy. Enitan took a bath to get some relief from the heat and then quickly settled to sleep because she had to report to work early the following day.

For many hours, Ade Bantan found it simply impossible to sleep due to the usual reasons: heat and mosquitoes. He often wondered why he didn't get feverish during the day as a result of prolonged bouts of insomnia. It was probably because he did nothing but lie on the couch all day long. He didn't spend his time trawling the streets during the blistering days in conditions condusive to developing fevers.

At dawn, Susan, having been awakened by Sumbo, came into the bedroom to prepare for her morning bath. Ade Bantan watched her through half-closed eyes while she took off her nightdress and picked up a tiny piece of soap and her toothbrush. He never tired of sneaking a peak at the under-aged striptease. It struck him as a bit of harmless paedophilia. A little assemblage of imagery to keep the fire of the imagination alive. It was a little secret he had discovered in a minute corner of dawn, a trinket he had taken without having it given or his having asked. Susan returned to rub body lotion on her body.

As usual, Enitan was still sleeping. In the living room Toscin and Waddadah were still lying on the floor so Sumbo couldn't begin her daily chore of cleaning. Papa Osaze could be heard in the middle of a fervent prayer session. Handclapping and drumming emanated from the white garment church down the street. Tin cups and pans clattered in the kitchens. Street vendors were busy adding their own sounds to the raucous cacophony of noises. Motorcycles had their engines revved up and cars sped past. The day had begun. Still, Ade Bantan couldn't come up with ways to to employ his time gainfully.

Waddadah got up about twenty minutes after Susan had left for school, and told Sumbo she was leaving. Sumbo wanted to go in and fetch Enitan, but Waddadah told her not to bother. Sumbo woke up Enitan so she could sweep the bedroom. Enitan emerged from the bedroom yawning and carrying a piece of soap in her hand.

Where is Waddadah?

She's gone.

She couldn't even say goodbye?

She didn't want her to disturb you.

What more disturbance can she cause me after having to accommodate her? Anyway I'm sure she'll come back again soon.

When Enitan finished having her bath and had gotten ready for work, Ade Bantan saw her off to the bus stop. Shortly after he returned, Sumbo left for her place of work and Toscin went off for her own engagement. Ade Bantan was left alone to cope with the travails of another hot, empty day. He flitted in and out of consciousness and chased off flies when he had the will. He tried not thinking of what Enitan might be doing. He tried not thinking about the consequences of sloth. He tried hard to ignore the mustiness that threatened to engulf him. He tried in vain to at least attain a negative state of nirvana.

As he managed to endure the long wait before sundown, Ulmanmadu breezed in, saying he was hungry. Ade Bantan told him he didn't know what was left in the kitchen and told him to go ahead to check if he didn't mind. Ulmanmadu went off and emerged a few minutes later with a cold dish of noddles, which he ate with his fingers as he talked.

This food is very cold.

Why didn't you warm it up on the stove.

I was too hungry.

You shouldn't complain then.

When are these girls coming back?

Soon.

Where is Susan?

She's probably out in the courtyard behind playing with the other kids.

This is worse than dog food or chicken food.

But you're eating it.

I've got no choice. Have thought about the matter we spoke about the other time?

I am still giving it some thought. It is a good idea.

I always come up with good ideas. Everyone knows that. And the fact that you're with our sister puts you in a position to enjoy many of my good ideas. But I'm not just an ideas man. I have the brains and connections to make them work. Ideas by themselves are worthless. You've got to be able to back them with something extra; this makes a world of difference between ideas that remain floating the air and ideas that find life and form.

So what brings you to these parts?

I just miss you guys, that's all, and I wanted to give you another chance to appreciate the beauty of my face.

How considerate of you.

It is always a pleasure to give you guys a chance to appreciate genuine physical as well as inner beauty. Why is this place so quiet? I can't stand quiet places they just drive me crazy.

It seems silent now because no one is in.

I don't think I could ever live in this sort of place. I would just go mad. You should come to where we live. It is so full of life, everyone and everything jumping about. Money is changing hands, deals are being made at every sound, fools die each night by the thousands, and new millionaires are laughing all the way to the bank the following morning. Now that is life. That is how it should be. This place looks and feels like some village in the middle of nowhere. No enterprising young man should stay here. There's nothing happening here. It's just a waste of time trying to make good here. Only old people and retirees should hang out here waiting to die. You know what I mean? I'd like you to take our sister out of this dead zone once you get married.

I'll do what I can.

It is better for you guys to go to a place that is full of life.

So what are you doing with yourself these days?

I am a hustler. Once a hustler, always a hustler. I'll peddle shit as long as it will sell. I'll sell anything; monkey shit, dog shit, even lion shit if I can find a way to get it. The only thing I won't do is sell fresh human body parts. That has serious repercussions that many who do such business don't know. Yes, it's true we all want money, but there are spiritual forces that walk hand-in-hand with money that you have to contend with. These forces adore human blood and fight fervently over it. Is easy to be caught in the cross-fire when they are fighting over human blood. It is better to deal in dried human body parts because it has been drained of blood and is, therefore, no longer attractive to the spiritual forces. I hope you understand what I'm saying . . . anyway, if you don't, I'll understand, because I'm discussing what happens in the metaphysical realm. I'm talking about the seventh stratum to heaven. These are issues only Buddhists, believers of Hinduism, Seven Day Adventists, Friends, and Moonists would understand. I want to start my own spiritual sect because all sorts of pranksters are having a field day. I'm beginning to get totally sick of it. Those who haven't the faintest idea of spirituality are running the land. Tell me, can the blind lead the sick? I want you to answer me that. Of course not.

Susan dashed in from the corridor and asked for a plate of noodles that had been kept for her in the kitchen since morning. Neither Ade Bantan nor Ulmanmadu replied. She withdrew back into the corridor and started to cry. The men in the living room didn't know she had started to cry. Enitan returned early from work because she had been granted permission to go for a medical checkup. She found Susan weeping in the corridor and asked what was wrong. Susan told her someone ate the noodles that had been kept for her in the kitchen. Enitan stormed into the living demanding an answer for the missing noodles without acknowledging Ulmanmadu's greeting.

Who ate Susan's noodles? I want to know now.

Enitan you've hardly entered and already you're getting agitated.

Of course I should be agitated when a poor girl is getting starved under my very nose. What ate her noodles?

I did.

You? Ulmanmadu? How could you? How can you deprive the poor little girl of her meal? This is totally unacceptable. I won't stand for this kind of rubbish. We don't do that sort of thing here. We respect other peoples' things before laying hands on them.

Ade Bantan, did he ask you for permission before he ate Susan's noodles?

He said he was hungry and wanted something to eat, so I told him to check in the kitchen for some food.

That isn't permission. He ought to have asked specifically for permission to eat Susan's noodles.

I told Ade Bantan I was hungry and he said I could go into the kitchen for some food.

That isn't the same thing as asking for permission. Now the poor girl is crying and starving and you stand there making useless excuses for yourself. I'm really disappointed in you. A grown man like yourself denying a poor little girl of her meal. This is totally annoying and heartbreaking. You should know how much I love that girl. I am ready to do anything for her. I take her like my own child and it just drives me mad to learn someone had the gaul to make her cry. I won't tolerate that kind of crap in any way. Where are Sumbo and Toscin?

Ade Bantan informed her that they were not yet back.

Where could those useless girls have gone now? I am starving as well. I want some food now and they are not here. They've started to behave like bosses. If they think now that they're bosses, they can leave and get their own apartments. What sort of inconsiderateness is this? I go to work and return to meet an empty house and no food on the table. This is total crap.

I'm sure they'll soon be back.

They better be! Susan, come and sit here by me on the floor and stop crying. There you go. Come and sit by me here. That's my girl. Good girl. So what are we going to do now, eh? No food has been prepared for us. You just wait until those girls return. I'll give them a good tongue lashing. You just wait and see.

After about ten minutes, Sumbo and Toscin entered the living room at the same time.

Where have you been?

Toscin asked me to accompany her to meet a man who was supposed to give some leads concerning job opportunities.

But why did you stay so long?

The traffic was very bad because there was rioting in the middle of town. Didn't you hear about it?

No. So what happened?

Motor park touts were rioting for increases over the amount they charged commercial bus drivers. They were burning tires right on the streets to stop cars from passing. They broke the windshields of drivers who resisted. Some of the drivers didn't even do anything to offend them. They just broke their windshields for the fun of it. It was terrible. Shops were looted and some were even burnt to ashes.

How about the police? What did they do?

Nothing. They didn't even bother to show up. At some moments, we feared for our lives. We had to pluck leaves and branches from trees as a mark of solidarity. Cars that had no leaves and branches were destroyed. Their owners were dragged down and kicked and slapped around. At that point, I felt glad that I had no car. My dear sister, we saw hell.

Can you please get me and Susan something to eat?

Hasn't Susan eaten? I made some noodles for her in the morning so that she could have something to eat this evening.

Ulmanmadu has eaten her noodles. I was very angry with him.

So what would you like to eat now?

Some noodles would do. Can you send Susan to get some in one the shops around?

No problem.

Thanks.

Susan come and get some money for your noodles.

Thank you.

As Susan was going out, Bisi Bala, an old friend of Enitan, entered with her eight-year-old daughter, Bintu. Bisi Bala was a freelance copy writer still struggling to make ends meet. She came in from time to time when she had accommodation problems. But she mostly came alone and not with her daughter. She carried a small handbag so it didn't appear that she intended to stay for long.

Hi Enitan. Wow! You have a full house. I hope I'm not disturbing anything?

Come and sit down, please. How are you and how goes your work? Bintu, come and say hello to me. You're a big girl now.

Gee I'm so exhausted. Can I have some water?

Toscin, please can you give Bisi Bala a glass of water?

Thank you, my darling.

So what's up Bisi? What brings you here this night.

My friend, it's a long story. My mother is in one of her terrible moods again. This time around, she didn't only throw me out. She threw out her granddaughter as well.

What happened? What did you do to make her angry this time?

She wanted me to increase Bintu's monthly food allowance.

And why didn't you? Don't you know how expensive things are nowadays? You don't pay rent to her, so you might as well try to help out by stocking up the house with food.

But where is the money Enitan? You're talking as if you don't know what it means to survive in this wretched city. You know how much I work my butt off just to get by and nothing seems to be working. I haven't bought myself a decent dress for two years just so I can pay for Bintu's school fees. I have to buy her school uniform and pay for her healthcare. I have to do everything by myself. Her father is nowhere to be found and his family doesn't do anything for Bintu.

So how long do you want to stay here?

I just want a little time to get my shit together and move on. I know I owe you some big favors and somehow, I hope to pay back someday. I really appreciate what you've done for me.

Are you guys hungry?

It would be nice to have something to eat before we sleep.

Enitan called for Sumbo to make some pap and vegetable stew for Bisi and Bintu. Sumbo brought the food in about half an hour. The living room barely had a spare inch left. Ulmanmadu was sitting in a corner, still piqued from Enitan dressing him down. Ade Bantan was lying in his usual position on the couch. Enitan was sitting on the floor with Susan beside her. Bisi and Bintu sat on another part of the floor directly in front of the television set. Toscin lay in the space between the couch and the wall. Sumbo didn't find any room to squeeze into, so she kept puttering around in the kitchen. She packed all the used dishes into a basin, which she placed in the cupboard. She would try and get Toscin to wash them tomorrow morning. She only hoped Toscin would agree. Toscin was lazy and Sumbo had to do most of the shopping, cooking, and cleaning. Toscin shirked doing any chores by chatting with Chidi's mother and sisters.

While Sumbo cleared the dirty dishes away, Enitan and Ade Bantan went into the bedroom. They couldn't sleep yet because Sumbo and Toscin had to change into their night clothes. Both girls were very skilled in undressing in the midst of people. When you lived in crammed and congested places, it was one of the first things you learned to do. They both felt quite comfortable in undressing in Ade Bantan's presence. Ulmanmadu removed his shirt and trousers, leaving only his boxers, and made space for himself on the couch. The couch was not really comfortable. It was only four feet long and had hard cushions. Ade Bantan's neck ached from lying on it for long periods. Bisi and Bintu slept in the same clothes they had worn throughout the day. In less than two hours, everyone had settled in their places. Enitan and Ade Bantan slept with the light on because they knew that someone might need to fetch something during the night. It felt doubly hot in the living room because more people were sleeping there.

At dawn, Bisi woke up Bintu and brought out her school uniform from her stuffed duffle. Bisi Bala instructed her daughter to brush her teeth and helped in combing her hair. Neither Bisi nor Bintu had a bath because they hadn't brought a towel or soap along. After dropping off Bintu at school, Bisi didn't return to Enitan apartment. Instead, she went on her usual rounds of business offices looking for freelance work. She avoided going to the apartment even though she would have liked to, because she didn't want to get into anybody's way. She had already made a nuisance of herself as it was.

As Sumbo cleaned the living room, she smelled the stench of urine on the spot where Bintu had slept. She kept this to herself because she knew Enitan would flare up. After a few days, Bisi and Bintu started getting comfortable living there. On a couple of days, Bisi came in early for some late lunch prepared by Sumbo. She didn't go visiting any friends in the evening but remained in the flat instead. Bintu's bedwetting, or rather, floor-wetting, became a daily occurrence. Sumbo didn't have to tell Enitan; everyone could smell the strong odor of urine pervading the entire apartment.

Who has been pissing here? asked Enitan one morning after Bisi had taken Bintu to school.

Your friend's daughter.

This is absolutely disgusting. What kind of thing is this? We are all going to chased away from this apartment because of the smell of piss. Has she offered to clean the carpet?

She pretends not to know her daughter has been peeing on the floor.

I'm going to send her packing when she come back. I don't even know what sort of woman she is. She doesn't have her bath in the morning and hardly changes her clothes. How can anyone give her any business when she is always looking unkempt? I wouldn't give such a tramp any business. I know she is honest and whatnot. But that is not enough. I don't even believe she has had a change of underwear since she's been here. The same applies to her pisshead of a daughter.

There must be something troubling the girl. How can she continue to pee on the floor every night? Susan has never done that once in this place and now some little brat wants to chase us out of here with stale piss. Nonsense. I can't believe how some people behave. You give them an inch, they take a yard, you give them a yard, they take a mile. See what has happened now . . . I agree to accommodate her for a few days and she wants to use the stink of piss to drive me out of town. I will never let this happen. This is not my lot in life.

Hankpaun came into to invite Sumbo and Ade Bantan to her engagement party. Ade Bantan was lying on the couch in a skimpy orange pair of shorts and nothing else.

How are you guys this morning? asked Hankpaun.

Not bad except for the smell of piss.

The smell of piss? What's that?

A friend's daughter has been pissing on my carpet every night.

How come?

I am accommodating my friend Bisi Bala and her daughter for a few days and now they want to drive us out of our own apartment with the smell of piss.

I see what you mean. How sad.

This is bad.

Sorry about your problems. Anyway, the reason I've come over is to invite you and Ade Bantan to my engagement party.

So soon?

Yes, we want to get it over with as soon as possible.

So when is it?

This weekend.

What time?

It begins at two-thirty in the afternoon at Alakyia-Gamson Memorial College at Kilometer 42.

Ade Bantan wasn't wearing underwear and his prodigious manhood had spilled out of the edge of his skimpy orange shorts. Hankpaun could see his display, but was too embarrassed to comment or ask him to sit properly. Enitan noticed that Hankpaun was looking uneasy, but couldn't figure out why. Rather than keep looking at Ade Bantan's shorts, Hankpaun turned her gaze away. Finally, Enitan looked at Ade Bantan's shorts and saw what had been causing Hankpaun's discomfort.

Ade Bantan, sit properly! We can all see your family jewels! No wonder Hankpaun has been looking funny. Hankpaun, why didn't you say something?

Hankpaun was too embarrassed to even answer the question. Ade Bantan rearranged himself properly back into his shorts and adjusted himself on the couch to avoid a reccurrence. Hankpaun soon left for work. Enitan fumed for a while and said that she would have pointed it out to Hankpaun's man if it had been her. Ade Bantan couldn't understand why she was more concerned about his exposed cock than he was. He was slightly embarrassed, but viewed the episode as one of those common moments of embarrassment that could happen to anybody.

Enitan had her bath and then he saw her to the bus stop. Another hot vacant day was only beginning to yawn and stretch out before Ade Bantan. He hoped the weekend would arrive quickly so he could attend Hankpaun's get-together. It should be a considerable change from lying on a couch everyday with an exposed dick. He would hear different noises and music, see some dancing, and see some new faces. That should definitely be a change.

At midday, when he could no longer stand the heat, Ade Bantan went for a cold bath. The water itself was lukewarm because its storage had been touched by the sun. He was glad to find himself alone after the assault to his senses caused by Ulmanmadu's visit. Ulmanmadu seemed to go on about everything ceaselessly. There was no respite once he got going on any anything.

Soon after Ulmanmadu's departure, Ade Bantan started to sweat again. He couldn't go anywhere under the blazing sun. It was hard to think or do anything constructive. He could only quietly await sundown or wish for some rain. It struck him that it hadn't rained for a long time. He wondered why. He couldn't immediately think of one reason. As he was thinking about what more he could do to get some relief from the heat, Joshua entered into the living room clutching a traveling bag over his right shoulder. He had come university on a short break.

Good to see you . . . how was your journey and how is your program coming along?

Everything is great, thank you.

We did know you would be coming today and that is why none of your sisters is here.

So what can I offer you?

I would like a cool beer.

Great, let me put on my shirt.

Where are we going?

Oh we'll just go to a nearby drinking joint.

I think we should wait for one of my sisters to come back.

Ok, that is fine by me. But I must warn you, it's terribly hot in here.

No problem. I'll survive.

Good strong man. I like that kind of talk. So tell me, how was your trip?

Terrible.

What happened?

I am sure that you are aware there are ritual killers everywhere. They go about killing people for body parts; penises, breasts, hearts, and vaginas. These killers then sell these parts to traditional medicine men who use them for money-making rituals. It is going on everywhere, I'm sure you must have heard about it.

Sure I've heard some things about ritual killings and that kind of shit.

Well this was what happened. I boarded this bus on the highway because I didn't have money to go to a bus station. You see, the fares are cheaper if you catch a bus on the highway. So this station wagon stopped by me and I was told to get inside. I looked inside and saw a driver and a guy in front beside him, two guys at the last row of seats at the back, and two women on the middle row. So I sat with the women at the middle and we began the journey. The guys at the back looked mysterious, you know, like people who live by incantations in dark, shady places. I can't really explain how they looked, but what I can say is that they weren't the normal kind of guys you see everyday if you know what I mean. And then I noticed there were two rams in the trunk at the back. Their horns were poking out and I could make out their heads. Then the driver turned off the highway. Heaven knows where the hell he was going. I started to turn around and look at the men at the back in their faces to let them know I was alert and that I wasn't sleeping. The rams would bleat from time-to-time, probably because they were squashed in the trunk. One of the medicine men at the back cocked his head as if he was about to strike me. So I kept looking back at him every now and then to make him know that it wouldn't be easy taking me out. All the while, we were making down this really deserted stretch of road that I couldn't for the life of me tell where it was leading. So, I began a song saying that my blood is black and bitter, and that it would jump around even when I die. I sang that I know the date of my death and it isn't going to be today. I think that was what put them off trying to slaughter me like a three-month-old goat. I think there and then they decided that my spirit wouldn't yield to the rituals they had intended to perform. You see my blood and spirit have got to yield themselves up, but my internal energy was contrary to their plan; and so that is why they decided not to kill like a cheap Christmas goat. My song showed that I was in the know about what they planned to do to me. Once you let them know that, then their plan is ruined. They would have to find another death head to use for their rituals.

That was a really close shave.

You can say that again. I was almost shitting myself. I can never forget the features of the medicine man behind me who cocked his head as if he were about to strike me. He was a cross between an albino and a redhead and he had freckles all over his face. At one point, he seemed to fall sleep and his big fat head sank into his broad chest and you won't believe it, he started to drool. I was amazed. And you know the funny part, none of the women beside me woke him up. They were all part of the same crew, as I was to discover. They were a team including the driver, and I was the only outsider among them. I was really very lucky.

You were. These ritual killings for money are getting out of hand. So now it's getting impossible to catch a ride on the highway with all those ritual murderers prowling the length and breadth of our causeways. It's really distressing. Would you like a shower or something?

Yeah, and I need to sleep as well, and then we can go for a beer. How about that? Oh! One other thing. Please don't tell my sisters about my experience with those bloody ritual killers . . . it would get them unduly worried and they would make me go to church for sessions of fasting and prayers and all that and I'm not ready for that kind of shit. I just want to chill out and enjoy myself.

No problem. Sounds great.

Joshua entered the bedroom and dumped his bag on an untidy pile of clothes. He unbuttoned his soaked shirt and took off his grungy jeans and boxers. He pulled a sheet from the unmade mattress and tied it around his slim waist and then wore Enitan's slippers, which were lying beside the mattress. He looked around for some soap and found a piece in the bowl where it was kept along with a tube of toothpaste. He had a shower and then slumped on the mattress inside the bedroom and promptly fell asleep. Ade Bantan managed to get some sleep too on the couch. Toscin woke them up as the sun was setting when she returned from her part-time job. Susan had returned, too, but was out playing with her friends around the yard. Toscin gave a little scream when she found Joshua sleeping inside and shook him awake.

Joshua, Joshua, when did you arrive? Long time no see! We've been expecting you to turn up anytime now. Why did you stay away so long before you decided to show up? How are you and everything?

I'm fine sis, so what's up?

I'm fine. I just returned from work, and look who I find here. What a surprise! No one downstairs told me that you had arrived.

I sneaked in and no one saw me. I just wanted to come for a short visit since it's been so long since I last saw you guys. So how is work? You must be a big girl at your place of work now.

I've only just started and you know what the economy is like. Everyone is just taking about emigrating and leaving this forsaken place. I'm getting tired of struggling myself. Nothing seems to work and it is so, so, so difficult to make any sort of headway here. I can tell you that. Things are tough.

You can say that again. I haven't had a decent meal for more than two months. I mean it's simply crazy. Can you believe that I haven't eaten a single good meal in more than two fucking months?

What would you like to eat my dear?

What have you got?

Not much, but enough to make you smile.

I hope so. I could eat a horse.

Tell me what would you like to eat.

I feel like eating something heavy.

How about fufu and vegetable stew?

That sounds great.

Wait here and let me make it for you then.

Thanks sis.

Always a pleasure.

Toscin stood up from the edge of the mattress where she had been sitting and went to the kitchen. In thirty minutes time, Toscin brought back a tray with Joshua's food. On seeing her emerging through the door frame he got up and clapped his hands in delight.

Well done my dear. Ha just what I need.

There you go. Enjoy!

Thanks sis… you're such a darling.

Have you guys been sleeping for long?

Quite long I would say. I was very tired. This semester has been really hectic for me. Lectures all through the day and then you have to write countless term papers and then you have those continuous assessment regulations whereby attendance is noted and all that shit. You'll soon be in varsity yourself, and then you'll see what I mean. It isn't easy to get a degree my sister.

You forget I'm a woman and I have the natural charms women have.

Yeah that's true but I expect you to go through the normal route to get your degree.

What is the normal route?

Hard work.

Fuck that bro. It isn't worth it. Everything is already fucked up. Period.

I agree with you. But all the same, I don't believe any of my sisters should go along that sort of route.

Look whose talking. You're not a softie yourself, so why are you talking like a priest? Besides, priests, as we all know, are no saints.

I'm not ready to argue now sis. Please let me eat first.

Please go ahead and enjoy yourself. I'll go and clean up the kitchen.

Thanks again sis.

Before Toscin left for the kitchen, Ade Bantan yawned and stretched.

How are you uncle? I've just been talking to Joshua. He said both of you have been sleeping for sometime? You must have been very tired.

Yes! The mosquitoes and the heat don't allow me to sleep at night, so I have to try to catch whatever bit of sleep I can during the day and forget about sleeping at night.

Lucky you. Those of us who have to work don't have the liberty to sleep during the day. In my place of work, it would be the surest way to career suicide. I think I should become an artist like you.

You don't become one just like that. You either are one or you're not and it's as different as night and day.

I see what you mean. Are you ready to eat now?

That would be nice.

Ok, I'll go and fetch your meal.

Thanks.

Toscin went into the kitchen and fixed Ade Bantan's meal. Sumbo returned from work and was delighted to see Joshua. Susan jumped on him clinging to his neck when she came in after hours of playing in the courtyard with other kids.

Enitan returned from work early because she had to prepare for a dinner appointment with a client. She was glad to see Joshua, but also somewhat apprehensive because he always made ceaseless demands for money. She was solely responsible for his tuition and was always complaining that the fees for his education would kill her. They were always having arguments that centered around him not getting enough and her being sent to an early grave because of his insatiable monetary needs.

Enitan's mood sank. The entire world seemed bent on dragging her down. She paid the rent for the apartment without the assistance of any of her siblings. She paid for the groceries and the toiletries. She paid the electricity bill. She paid for incidental medical bills. She paid for Susan's school fees and would have to fork out the money for Toscin's tuition. She paid for entertainment on public holidays and festive seasons. Their relatives came around and she paid for their amusement. She had to do everything by herself. She had a lover who couldn't assist her financially and she even had to push him as well to focus seriously upon his work.

Everyone took from her and none of them gave anything in return. Friends came off the streets and dumped their problems on her while she had to cope with her own hardships and obstacles by herself. She was getting very tired, she was feeling drained by the treadmill of people, demands, and giving. She needed some respite; she needed some kind of breakthrough from this endless sentence of suffering and deprivation.

Enitan looked around her crammed bedroom and it didn't feel as if it was hers. She didn't even notice Joshua's bag perched on the pile of rumpled clothes. What caught her eye was the tray of leftovers by the mattress. The room barely had any space left for her feet and now she now had to try and make her way around a mess of food scraps. She called for Toscin to take the tray to the kitchen. She sighed and wondered when her days of fruitless struggle would be over. If only Ade Bantan would put together a credible portfolio of work and fly her to Europe. That would make a huge difference in her life. As she was exploring this line of thought, she heard Bisi Bala come in with her daughter Bintu. This was the time to chuck her and her pisshead of a daughter out of this apartment.

Hi, Bisi Bala. How was your day?

Fine thank you.

Have you met my brother Joshua? He's just returned from varsity for a short break. So we have more than a full house now.

Yes, I met him. Welcome.

Bisi, you know how things are when the apartment is this full. No one is ever comfortable in this state, so I'd appreciate it if you would find an alternative arrangement tonight.

Tonight? Why so soon?

I told you. My brother is now here, and it's difficult to do anything here when the apartment is so full. I mean, I lose my things and other people complain about missing personal items and whatnot. It isn't convenient anymore.

But we all managed when Ulmanmadu was here. So what's the big deal? Can't you help a friend who has fallen on hard times? Mind you, this is only a temporary situation. Things will change. You'll see. So please, I'm asking you to bear with us for a little more time, at least until such time as my mother would be ready to take Bintu back in. I don't have a problem leaving, but it's Bintu. I want her to be at a place near her school so that she can be there on time and not have to go through unnecessary hardship at this very young age. That's my problem.

You don't seem to be listening to what I am saying. We are just too many in this tiny apartment and it isn't just possible to live like this any longer.

But I'm asking you as a friend to bear with me for only a few days.

And I'm telling you I can't! The entire apartment is stinking of your daughter's piss.

So that's what this is all this is about? I suspected something was the matter. All this was bothering you and you kept it from me? This is something we could have discussed and settled amicably.

I have had enough Bisi Bala. I need my space.

Ok, we'll go. Bintu, go and fetch our bags in the bedroom and let us leave.

Bye bye. Have a good evening.

So you're just going to throw a friendship of so many years away just because you can't be a bit more patient?

I've said my mind and that's that.

I really believe you're a heartless person. You're really mean. You don't have a child of your own; that's why you're annoyed simply because a girl peed overnight. This is really mean of you.

Please leave my apartment now, I've had enough of your crap.

I am disappointed in you. I had thought you were a friend; I didn't realize you're just a good time girl.

Just leave my apartment. I've had enough of your insults.

We are leaving. We too have had enough of your meanness and hypocrisy. In fact, I can't stand anyone who can't stand children. So this is what all this is about? My child? What has my child done to you? She's only a child and she's innocent. What has my poor innocent child done to you Enitan?

Bisi Bala I don't want to keep repeating myself on this issue; leave my house right now.

We are leaving; just let my poor daughter fetch our things.

How long with that take? I've had enough of your nonsense.

You see? You have no patience.

Thank you, but I don't need you to tell me that.

Bisi Bala and Bintu left the apartment in a defiant mood and Enitan went to the balcony to watch them go. She was peeved that Bisi Bala hadn't appreciated the few days she had allowed them to spend with her. She shouted from the balcony that she never wanted to see Bisi Bala again, hissed, and returned to her apartment. She tried to put the incident behind her so that she could prepare for her dinner with her client.

Enitan told Ade Bantan that she was going out to dinner with a client and he asked her if the client was male or female. She replied that he was male and Ade Bantan returned to the magazine he was reading. After a few moments, he looked up and asked if he might accompany her and she told him he couldn't because it was a business dinner. Enitan went into the bathroom to freshen up for her appointment. When she came back from the bathroom, Ade Bantan didn't go into the bedroom with her to watch her apply make-up as he usually liked to do. He wasn't very comfortable with the idea of her going alone on a dinner appointment with a male client at night.

It occurred to Ade Bantan that there was a world out there in which Enitan operated that he knew virtually nothing about. He knew nothing of how her work place operated and her place within its structure in terms of how she related with her co-workers and bosses alike. Since he lived his life mainly on a weather-worn couch, he couldn't form a reasoned opinion about the kind of world she trawled each day apart from the fragments she revealed to him, which he knew were bound to be selective and often distorted. She often forgot what she told him and never bothered to find out what impact her causal revelations made on him.

She had told him that during the course of their on-off relationship, she had had nine other lovers. He counted at least nine. And then, she constantly reminded him that she wasn't "loose in the arse." He didn't understand her definition of being loose in the arse. Nine lovers during a period of ten years or so. That she had had at least one new lover every year for a period of about ten years. By her own admission. And how about one-night stands? She didn't say anything about them. What was also troubling was that she didn't remember some of the most cherished memories of their long relationship. She couldn't recall the type of bed he had in his bedroom. She couldn't recall what kind of furniture he had. He could remember the mirror she spent hours in front of examining the appearance or non-appearance of wrinkles on her face and body. She couldn't remember the first day they made love. Meanwhile he remembered vital details of their relationship. He remembered the color, style, and texture of her lingerie from ten years back. He could remember the fragrance she wore and how it suited her. He remembered the restaurants and wine bars they frequented at the early stages of their affair. He remembered some of her favorite hairstyles. Her remembered her favorite hair stylists and hair care products. How could he ever forget such indelible details? He remembered how she ate and how she sat with him when they ate. He remembered her closest friends. He remembered the interior décor of their apartments. Perhaps interior décor was a trifle highfalutin—internal arrangement was more like it. He could recall the parties they went to together, the dances he was trying to master, and her peculiar styles of dance. He could recall some of her sexiest party clothes. He remembered exactly what her skin tone was like when she was twenty. He could recall the sort of jokes she liked. He knew her deepest desires and the ambitions that drove her to extremes.

What particularly bothered him was that Enitan often confused him with some of her previous lovers. How can one really trust someone who couldn't recall the deepest imprints of what is supposed to be her most life-changing relationship? If indeed their relationship was life-changing as she sometimes claimed it to be, why would she forget the treasure trove of their common memory bank?

Once Enitan had asked Ade Bantan why he didn't want to have a baby with her now. She said he had once been keen on having children and now he had changed, suddenly not interested in having kids. She told him that early in their relationship he insisted on not using condoms so she could get pregnant. She said she could recall him residing in a darkish apartment with heavy dark brown curtains. But he knew he never lived in a darkish apartment with dark brown curtains. She said she could recall them fucking a lot in his apartment, which had the feel of a decadent grotto. On his part, he could recall them fucking a lot, but in apartment that was airy and was filled with light, a sharp contrast with the darkish underground den of iniquity she so eloquently described. She mentioned that they usually fucked in the missionary position and that he would push her limbs against the head of the bed and hold her down until the last drop of semen had sunk into her womb. She said it was his way of ensuring that he got her pregnant, but she never did unfortunately. Ade Bantan could not recall ever wanting her to get pregnant. It simply wasn't true.

Instead, Ade Bantan had had visions of them leading a life of artistic experimentation and fulfillment. A life filled with much global travel and visits to the most exotic beaches. A life filled with much sunlight and freedom as opposed to a life of mediocrity, bourgeois mundanity, and eventually sub-bourgeois penury, shame, and viciousness.

Ade Bantan's vision of creativity, genial sunlight, and freedom was too far-fetched for even him to keep in mind, because it was difficult to connect it with the realities of

Enitan's present situation. She was bogged down with the demands and problems of raising her siblings and ministering to their every need. She couldn't sacrifice her commitment to them for any notion of imaginary pleasure. She simply didn't have the heart and imagination to take such a step.

Ade Bantan wanted to lead a productive life associated with the most fashionable art galleries, which would serve as a platform to communicate to the world the images that simultaneously frightened and gave him pleasure. He had thought Enitan would be able to come along with him on his selfish—nonetheless supremely creative—journey of adventure and self-discovery. He hadn't anticipated that her powers, inventiveness, and commitment would be tethered to a backstory that involved a host of siblings, relatives, friends, disappointments, and several articles of faith.

In the beginning, Enitan was rather skillful in concealing that part of her life from him. She led him to believe that hers was a journey of exploration and that greater consciousness seeking was more or less feasible. What crap. Instead, he hadn't known that Enitan saw him as a means to bring her cumbersome backstory up-to-date. He was the means by which the past and people she was dragging along could attain the desired kind of recognition. They never once had a showdown or an open confrontation as to whose vision of the future was tenable and therefore worth pursuing. Instead, like most relationships, a large amount of exploratory space was left to probe the desirability as well as the possibilities of compromise. In this case, compromise had been replaced by inertia, and then deception, and eventually outright conquest.

Had Ade Bantan remained in the purgatory of compromise, it was most certain that Enitan would have defeated him given his innate tendency to apathy and inertia. There was no doubt that her vision of their possible future together was fast gaining ground over his ill-communicated aspirations. He had succumbed to a chronic bout of inertia and Enitan had become his only hope of ever getting out of the tunnel in which he had found himself. She was the one who kept insisting that he wasn't in a tunnel and that he had much to offer in every sense. He felt highly flattered by her robust confidence in him.

Recently, he felt something had been extinguished with him, but he could only confess and confirm this depressing piece of information to himself. He could not attempt to tell anyone else. Not even Enitan, who had become the only credible and potent source of opposition to the silently creeping flood of inertia that was overtaking him. For providing him with this invaluable resource as well as opportunity, he ought to be forever indebted to her. He felt sure that she was unaware of how much of his life was in her hands. He hoped she never found out.

Nonetheless, it was rather disconcerting to Ade Bantan that Enitan confused memories of their many shared experiences together with those of her numerous other lovers. It made it difficult to give her what was really due to her in terms of gratitude, sincerity, and appreciation. He wished he could come up with an acceptable reason for her disturbing lapses of memory. On another occasion, she had mentioned that she remembered the times they spent watching movies and cartoons together in his bedroom. But he had never had a DVD player in his bedroom. In fact, as a matter of principle, he never watched movies in his bedroom. Moreover, he had never watched the movies and cartoons she claimed they watched together. He just couldn't make sense of most of the memories she associated with him.

Enitan got dressed and left for her dinner appointment when the client hooted his car horn signifying it was time to go. She looked stunning in her tight-fitting black slacks and matching black satin top. Her skin glowed against the backdrop of black.

Joshua came in and reminded Ade Bantan of their plan to visit a bar. Ade Bantan needed to go out even more now to keep from thinking of unsavory things about Enitan. She hadn't even bothered to give him a kiss when she left, and that disturbed him. He felt she ought to have done more to pacify his troubled heart. How could she have been so heedless? Had she been so excited about her appointment that she didn't notice him in lying on the couch with a sullen face? Where were her priorities? Yeah, having a drink with Joshua was a very good idea. It provided an excellent opportunity to get intoxicated.

When the two men emerged onto the streets, many activities were still taking place. Handclapping and drumming was going on at the white garment church. Commercial motorcyclists were making their riotous way across a maze of people, potholes, and paths. Traders had set up their makeshift stalls for a long night of trading and haggling. Roadside tea sellers had arranged their tables and benches for worn-out customers who came for tea, bread, butter, and eggs. Peddlers of bootleg gin hailed derelict figures from the fringes and shadows. Masked night-soil men went around to buildings collecting buckets of shit. Those who had a bit of change to spare were laughing noisily, trying to create the impression that things weren't that terrible. Beautiful women who really had no where to go were walking up and down the street pretending they had dates to keep.

Ade Bantan and Joshua reached an open-air drinking joint called *Shade's Point*, where the merry-making took place right in the middle of a road that was more alley than street. It was a dirt thoroughfare ridden with rubbish and loose rocks. Joshua liked to go there sometimes because it was spacious. It was possible to sit without brushing against the next person. It was possible to inhale something resembling air. During the day, it was not possible to have open-air drinking sessions, as motorists and motorcyclists congested the alley. *Shade's Point* was no more than a little spot during the day. It was a scruffy little kitchen where Shade, the proprietress, made catfish soup with chilli. Her catfish soup was the main attraction of the bar. After intense bouts of beer drinking, the chilli in the catfish soup had the effect of minimizing the damage done by alcoholic excess.

Shade, who was dark, tall, and imposing, also had a peaceful, unassuming mien, which was another strong selling point of the bar. Usually bar owners had to be as tough as they come because they had to deal with hardened armed robbers, common thieves, and coarse, loose women. Shade somehow managed to navigate this menagerie of criminal elements with considerable degree of skill and panache. She knew how to deal with characters who drank when they had no money. She also knew how to cope with the problems associated with adulterous men and women who used her place as a secret rendezvous. Many years of plying this trade had taught her to cope with most of these kinds of issues. What mattered at the end of day was that she had to ensure enough returns were coming so she had something to buy and sell the following day.

Ade Bantan and Joshua walked casually to Shade's place and stopped in the middle of thoroughfare where there were gatherings of people drinking. Shade went to a spot in front of her kitchen and removed two white plastic chairs from a stack. With the help of her sole waitress, she also carried a plastic table to where the men stood waiting. Both were smoking cigarettes and seemed unconcerned with what was going on around them. This was their neighborhood after all, and they had no reason to be apprehensive.

There were about fifteen people sitting around five tables. The mood of the place was buoyant. Ade Bantan wanted to stay at least a meter from the nearest table so he could at least have the chance to hear the timber of his own voice above the rising din. He and Joshua sat down in a slightly darker spot because it was shielded from the moonlight. Two large bottles of beer were brought before them and opened by Shade's waitress. The drinks were warm because the electricity was out. Ade Bantan ordered two bowls of catfish soup. Shade informed them that they would have to be patient because she had only just started preparing a fresh pot. The two men smoked some cigarettes and drank more of their warm beer. Ade Bantan was somewhat surprised that the clouds of mosquitoes that danced at the edge of the sewers were not as dense at they usually were. It meant they wouldn't have to waste their energy slapping off the damned pests. Good thing.

Twenty minutes later, the waitress, a girl of about sixteen, brought two steaming-hot bowls of catfish on a tray and placed it on the lopsided table. Ade Bantan and Joshua took final drags on their cigarettes and drank some beer to freshen up their taste buds. Joshua tasted his soup, his expression showing that he liked it. Ade Bantan took a few spoonfuls, but couldn't make out the flavor because it was so hot. After a couple more spoonfuls, his eyes started to roll back into his skull. He lost consciousness and fell off the chair. Commotion broke out. No one knew what had befallen him.

With Shade's assistance, Joshua got Ade Bantan up from the floor and managed to get him seated on the chair, with his head lolling sideways. Joshua was still collected enough to call Enitan on her cell phone to tell her that Ade Bantan had fainted. Some of the people drinking started leaving the place thinking that it maybe Ade Bantan would die and it would mean a lot of hassles for them if the cops started asking questions.

The young waitress ran to a major road two streets away and hailed a cab, directing the driver to Shade's joint. They took Ade Bantan to a derelict hospital located a little more than a kilometer from Enitan's apartment. By the time they were approaching the hospital, Ade Bantan had started to regain consciousness. Fortunately it wasn't a busy hospital, and he was admitted promptly. But no tests were conducted on him to find out what was wrong. The hospital didn't have the specialized equipment necessary to carry out such tests.

The hospital had only three workers on duty: a woman at the reception desk and two nurses dressed in drab blue uniforms. The single-story ediface was located on an incline, so the building itself looked and felt lopsided. In front of the building were had untended shrubs and plants covered with soot. Inside, on the hospital's walls, were cobwebs, which made its dark gloomy interior look like the depot of a failed business venture.

Neither Ade Bantan nor Joshua took in the woeful credentials of the medical practice. It was the hospital Enitan and her siblings patronized when they fell ill. The doctor in charge was a pudgy man with a potbelly. Dangling from his neck was an old stethoscope that didn't appear to be functional. Nothing seemed to function in the hospital. Dust covered the scanty furniture and floors. Dr. Bolo Mudini, the man attending to Ade Bantan, had six-day-old stubble on his face; he kept yawning and scratching his body.

Joshua explained to Dr. Mudini that he and Ade Bantan had both been eating catfish soup from the same supply when Ade Bantan had suddenly fallen off his chair. Dr. Mudini suggested that Ade Bantan might have been the victim of a case of food poisoning. If that were true, Joshua wondered aloud why he hadn't been affected. The doctor replied that it may have something to do with their different constitutions or genetic make-up. Joshua didn't feel satisfied with the casual answer but pressed him no further.

Ade Bantan was taken to a room, put on a drip and started on a course of antibiotics. His condition didn't seem critical and so Dr. Mudini hadn't had to strain his brain on what course of treatment to adopt. Thirty minutes later, Enitan arrived with her client, Levy Mopo Benzi, in tow. Benzi ran a company that packaged publicity events for large corporations. He needed Enitan's counsel on strategy for a series of events he was about to embark upon. He seemed impatient that his appointment with Enitan had been interrupted and was keen to resume their meeting.

Ade Bantan was rather concerned that Enitan seemed to be bowing to Benzi's pressures. She seemed eager to leave. Joshua let her know that the doctor still had no idea of what was wrong with Ade Bantan. Ade Bantan insisted that he needed her with him as his condition was still rather shaky. Enitan kept looking at Benzi with what seemed to Ade Bantan like a restiveness, longing and flirtatious. Why couldn't she stay with him in the hospital for the night? What if his condition grew worse during the course of the night and he passed on? Would she find the toughness of heart to forgive herself for her negligence and selfishness? Ade Bantan contemplated these questions as Enitan dwelled on the merits of resuming her appointment with Benzi.

Ade Bantan kept on insisting that he needed Enitan with him as his medical troubles were far from over. Besides, he didn't want to stay alone in a hospital that seemed strange and uninviting. Enitan replied that Joshua would be able to stay with him for the night. Ade Bantan pleaded that that wasn't the same as having his lover by his side as a source of strength and comfort.

Enitan's impatience to leave made Ade Bantan suspicious. What was she dealing with that couldn't be postponed? He was beginning to find her behavior rather unbecoming. Benzi's demeanor was even more unseemly. He kept insisting they leave as if he had the authority to decide how Enitan and Ade Bantan spent their time. He said that Ade Bantan looked all right and said that Enitan could always come back the following day.

Ade Bantan felt insulted by Benzi's presumptiveness. He had the audacity to comment on Ade's health without the merest acquaintance with him. He kept insisting on taking Enitan away at an hour that was far past normal business hours of operation. But Benzi's insistence wasn't barbaric. Instead, it was coated with what appeared to be an insidious kind of charm. He smiled all the time and he didn't utter crude words. But his entire manner was offensive. What was most rude was his devious way of asserting himself. Nonetheless, Ade Bantan kept insisting that Enitan stay by his bedside for the night. Eventually, she agreed to remain and Benzi had to go off by himself. Ade Bantan was pleased his will had triumphed. Joshua, who had stood back while the tussle ensued, left ten minutes later.

The night in the hospital wasn't pleasant. Ade Bantan sweated profusely as he drained the drip. By morning, his mysterious ailment had disappeared just as suddenly as it had appeared. After Dr. Mudini presided over his discharge, he and Enitan emerged from the gloomy hospital into the midst of a bright and vibrant day. They hailed a taxi cab and headed to Enitan's apartment. Sumbo, Toscin, and Susan had already gone out by the time they entered the apartment. Joshua was lying on the floor listening to music from the radio. Enitan dashed into the room, took off her clothes, and then made for the bathroom. She was due at her office and already late. Minutes later, she was back in the bedroom dressing up for work. On that morning, Ade Bantan didn't watch her apply her make-up, but lay on the couch instead, chatting with Joshua. But when Enitan was ready to leave, he saw her to the bus stand.

By the weekend, Ade Bantan was strong enough to attend Hankpaun's wedding engagement party. A day before the party, Enitan took Ade Bantan shopping so that he could have some proper clothes to wear. She selected a dashiki and pair of dress shoes for him at a boutique in a suburb. Hankpaun, in company of neighborhood friends including Enitan and Ade Bantan, organized a commercial bus to take them all to the school ground on which the party was taking place.

It was a bright sunny day. Tents-had been erected all over the field to protect guests from the glare of the sun and against possible rainfall. Enitan settled Ade Bantan into a chair underneath one of the tents and promptly disappeared. He felt lost. He hardly knew anyone at the party and no one came to his table to ask if he needed anything. Thirty minutes later, Enitan reappeared, apologizing for her tardiness. She said she was needed to help in serving the guests. She promised she would soon be back with his plate of food.

A live band was playing, but the vastness of the field made it impossible to have an inspiring acoustical impact. The band played mostly old highlife tunes and seemed to have been called upon to play as a last-ditch arrangement.

An hour and a half later, Ade Bantan still hadn't been served. He felt like leaving the field and going back to the apartment to stretch out on the couch if Joshua wasn't already on it. The problem was that the large field, which had been chosen because it was cheap, was far out of town and it wasn't not possible to get easy transportation back to town. Besides, Enitan held the purse and he had no money.

Some time later, Enitan returned with a cold plate of fried rice, lamb, and chicken. It provided no comfort to Ade Bantan because he had been fuming. But he tried as much as possible to hide his annoyance from Enitan.

Enitan threw her bag to Ade Bantan for safekeeping while she continued to go from tent to tent ministering to the needs of guests. Ade Bantan looked into her bag and saw a huge wad of cash. He brought out a quarter of it and slipped it into his pocket for use in case he chanced upon a vehicle going back into town. The band continued to emit sounds buffeted by winds and myriad noises. It was more of an annoyance than a harmless distraction. He refused a bottle of beer, which had been brought after numerous requests, because it was warm. The sodas tasted flat and flavorless because they were also warm. All he could do was wait until sunset to return home. He regretted having agreed to come.

At sunset, a group of about twenty people packed themselves in the bus with containers of leftover food and drinks. Some of the women had bawling toddlers on their backs. The driver of the bus was a stocky barrel-chested man. Enitan and Ade Bantan sat beside each other. The women had really come prepared for the party. Many of them wore colourful boubous of lace and striking headgear nearly a foot long. By sunset, their make-up had become undone, with grease and sweat running all over their faces. But they all seemed happy because they had had a great time. It had been an occasion to show off their new shoes and the latest headgear styles. It had been a time to get away from litters of children who made them yell by the minute. It had been a time to give their indifferent husbands stirrings of sexual arousal. It had been an occasion to remind themselves they were all once young girls who liked to laugh over simple things. It had been a moment to get away from the hassles involving constant increases in the price of groceries and the cheapest dried fish. The glow of their skin and their lucid eyes were a reminder that the power of escape and fantasy was a great healer or at least a balm to apply to get through yet another day. They all sat crammed in the bus as it sped in darkness toward the town. It was a forty-five minute drive back to town barring traffic.

Suddenly, the driver jammed hard on the brakes. A pile of wood had been stacked across the highway and there was no way around it. The impact of the act was considerable. People were thrown off their seats and hurled forward. Babies started to cry. Headgear flew off heads. The driver tried to reverse, and did begin to move, when gun-toting figures appeared from the bushes. The bus was trapped between a pile of stacked wood and five men with sub-machine guns. The women started to pray for their lives and those of their toddlers. The armed men casually surrounded the bus. Some of them were smoking pot, which they offered to some of the distraught women. None of them accepted. Then, an armed robber offered a joint to ten year old boy. The boy refused and got a resounding blow in his temple for his bravery. His mother started to cry. Some of the robbers laughed.

So you people have been having fun eh? What have you brought for us?

There is food and drinks. Please help yourselves, said a woman who sat in front beside the driver.

Thank you very much. You're so kind.

Two robbers pointed guns at the driver's head while the others brought out the containers of food and drinks and started to help themselves to the contents. They brought out every container of food. Then they asked the passengers on the bus to hand over all the money they had. Three of the robbers meticulously made mental notes of those who had money and those who didn't. Ade Bantan brought out the money he had taken out of Enitan's bag earlier. Enitan gave them the remaining cash she had with trembling hands.

Five of the passengers had no money to hand over. Perhaps they felt there was no need to carry any since the bus driver had already been paid before their trip. The robbers told these five, four women and one man, to get off the bus. Two of the women had toddlers with them. An armed robber yanked the toddlers from their arms and returned them to the bus, handing them over to be carried by a couple of the women who remained on the bus. Deprived of their mothers, the babies started to bawl loudly.

Outside, the five passengers were told to lie across the highway in a single file. Two robbers got into the bus and instructed the driver to move the bus in reverse. Then, with a gun pointed at his head, the robbers demanded that he drive over the heads of the passengers lying face down on the highway. Everyone started to scream but the robbers told them to stop or be shot, one-by-one. The driver hesitated, and the robbers held on tighter to the triggers of their guns. The other robbers helping themselves to the containers of food commanded him to step on the accelerator.

The bus jerked over the heads of the passengers as if it were moving over speed bumps. The sole man among the passengers got up and tried to run toward the bush. He got a bullet to the back of his head for his efforts. He slumped to the ground. He was shot a few more times in his back. At that, no one could scream. They had been ordered to remain silent upon pain of death.

Only the toddlers continued to wail. A robber grabbed them and placed them in each arm. Audible sighs of apprehension could be heard. The robber placed the two crying toddlers by a thicket of bush and shot both of them in their heads. Some of the passengers whose heads had been driven over were still twitching in the final throes of death. A robber went into the bush and brought out the getaway car where it had been hidden. Ade Bantan was instructed to get off the bus. He was ordered to assist the driver in stacking the logs behind the bus to delay its return to the town. The robbers kicked them constantly on their butts to make them hurry. The idea was to get the bus to face the direction it had been coming from before it was waylaid.

It was hard, strenuous work, but they had no choice. Guns were being trained on their backs. About fifteen minutes later, the robbers sped off to town. The women began to wail. It was terrible. The exhausted men who had just stacked the the logs atop one another had to began to throw them off the highway again. The bodies of passengers lying on the highway were also carried to the side of the road. The day of Hankpaun's party had turned into great tragedy, the details of which no one wanted to recall. No one spoke about it. No one wanted to remember.

Many days after Papa Osaze was supposed to deliver Enitan's car, it still hadn't arrived. He kept making excuses.

The customs officials who were supposed to oversee the project were on leave and hadn't come back. It wasn't yet safe to bring the car in because new border patrols had been launched. A spate of armed robberies prevented the arrival of the car. Enitan started to get impatient and her sisters were saying they had been duped. Papa Osaze asked them to give him one more week to deliver the vehicle.

Joshua had been hanging out with a friend from the neighborhood, whom everyone thought was gay. His friend, Larry K. Ghumphus, worked in an auditing firm as an accountant. He was fair skinned and not too tall. He had approached Joshua in a simple manner and he seemed honest and genuinely friendly. He also had a quiet charm that Joshua felt comfortable with. They went to the beachfront to have dinner on many occasions. As the walked by the beach, Larry would try to hold Joshua's hand, but he always withdrew. Larry never propositioned Joshua, but always loved to spend time alone with him. He constantly bought him presents and never failed to give such tender smiles. Joshua accepted Larry because he liked him and because he was generous and committed to their friendship.

Rumors had started to spread regarding what Joshua and Larry did when they were alone together on their numerous trips to the beachfront. Concerned neighbors warned Enitan, Sumbo, and Toscin that the much older Ghumphus was gay and that he was trying to seduce the apparently unwitting Joshua.

Enitan started to put pressure on Joshua to break off his relationship with Larry. Joshua asked her for a reason. She said because he was gay. Joshua replied that that wasn't a good reason. She threatened to stop paying his fees at the university. Only then did he began to withdraw from Larry K Ghumphus. Enitan asked once more if he had broken off their relationship. He replied that he had. She said she didn't believe him. One evening, when he came back from a stroll, all his sisters and their friend Hankpaun held hands, surrounding Joshua in the middle of the circle they formed. They walked around him in circles while they prayed for him. They were going to break his bond with Larry K Ghumphus using the power of female blood and spirit. Joshua wasn't amused, but there wasn't anything he could do. He soon went back to the university to continue with his academic program, putting a real distance between him and Larry K Ghumphus. Many years later, he regretted having yielded to the pressures of his sisters.

Since Enitan and her sisters started to mount pressure on Papa Osaze to deliver the car, his prayers had become more fervent. Enitan, her sisters, and Ade Bantan could distinctly hear every word Papa Osaze uttered in his never-ending prayer sessions. He prayed that all his enemies should fall down and die. He prayed that all those who were against his progress and his family's well-being should fall down and die. He prayed that those that couldn't stand to see him drive a more expensive car should fall down and die. He prayed that those who did not want to see him live in a bigger apartment with his family should fall down and fell. He prayed that those who said that his son Osaze had sex with his sister Angel should fall down and die. He prayed that those who claimed his wife was a vicious and uncaring mother should fall down and die. He prayed that those who called him an arrogant man should fall down and die. He prayed that those who branded him a thief and a con artist should fall down and die. He prayed that those who could not see his qualities as an anointed leader in the spiritual realm should fall down and die. He prayed that those who doubted his powers as a healer of the faithless and the dispossessed should fall down and die. Papa Osaze invariably launched into a prolonged incantatory phase that sounded like the feet of a dozen elephants pounding against the ground:

Die die die die die die die die die die die die die die die die
die die die die die die die die die die die die die die die die die
die die die die die die die die die die die die die die die die die
die die die die die die die die die die die die die die die die die
die die die die die die die die die die die die die die die die die
die die die die die die die die die die die die die die die die die
die die die die die die die die die die die die die die die die die
die die die die die die die die die die die die die die die die die
die die die die die die die die die die die die die die die die die
die die die die die die die die die die die die die die die die die
die die die die die die die die die die die die die die die die die
die die die die die die die die die die die die die die die die die
die die die die die die die die die die die die die die die die die
die die die die die die die die die die die die die die die die die
die die die die die die die die die die die die die die die die die
die die die die die die die die die die die die die die die die die
die die die die die die die die die die die die die die die die die
die die die die die die die die die die die die die die die die die
die die die die die die die die die die die die die die die die die
die die die die die die die die die die die die die die die die die
die die die die die die die die die die die die die die die die die
die die die die die die die die die die die die die die die die die
die die die die die die die die die die die die die die die die die
die die die die die die die die die die die die die die die die die
die die die die die die die die die die die die die die die die die
die die die die die die die die die die die die die die die die die
die die die die die die die die die die die die die die die die die
die die die die die die die die die die die die die die die die die
die die die die die die die die die die die die die die die die die

228

die die die die die die die die die die die die die die die die die
die die die die die die die die die die die die die die die die die
die die die die die die die die die die die die die die die die die
die die die die die die die die die die die die die die die die die
die die die die die die die die die die die die die die die die die
die die die die die die die die die die die die die die die die die
die die die die die die die die die die die die die die die die die
die die die die die die die die die die die die die die die die die
die die die die die die die die die die die die die die die die die
die die die die die die die die die die die die die die die die die
die die die die die die die die die die die die die die die die die
die die die die die die die die die die die die die die die die die
die die die die die die die die die die die die die die die die die
die die die die die die die die die die die die die die die die die
die die die die die die die die die die die die die die die die die
die die die die die die die die die die die die die die die die die
die die die die die die die die die die die die die die die die die
die die die die die die die die die die die die die die die die die
die die die die die die die die die die die die die die die die die
die die die die die die die die die die die die die die die die die
die die die die die die die die die die die die die die die die die
die die die

Everyone who lived in the compound began to call Papa Osaze by the name of Archbishop Die, as death was the main subject of all his prayers. Enitan was the first to call him by the moniker behind his back because her apartment was closest to his and so had to endure the awful drone of his prayers at close range. She also noticed that anytime she asked when her second-hand car would be delivered, the following morning, he would launch his invocations of death with greater ferocity. Papa and Mama Osaze's children, Osaze, Angel, Amber, and Blessing stopped visiting Enitan's apartment's to play.

When Enitan's vehicle was delivered, it was a broken-down piece of junk that had been freshly painted. It stopped working on its first test drive. Enitan was livid. She wanted her money back. Papa Osaze argued that he had delivered his part of the bargain and could do no more for her. That made Enitan even angrier. Their neighbors within the compound tried to intervene many times looking for a solution to the conflict. Neither Papa Osaze nor Enitan wouldn't budge. It seemed an ugly showdown was imminent.

Ade Bantan started to find it impossible to live with Enitan. All she ever thought about was getting her money back. They both went see Papa Osaze's group leader at his church premises. Enitan swore she would let everyone know that she had been duped by a so-called staunch spiritualist. She would let the world know that Papa Osaze was just another corrupt person employing the mask of religion to engage in nefarious activities.

At the church, which was where Papa Osaze attended with his family, his group leader kept them waiting for three hours because he was busy settling a case of fornication involving an usherette and a church messenger. The allegation was that the acts of sexual congress were committed in the wee hours of the morning at the back of the church building. When the group leader was finally ready to see Enitan and Ade Bantan, he was clearly exhausted and could only promise to look into the matter. Days passed and they didn't hear a word from the church group leader. Enitan decided to try another approach. She headed to the police and enlisted the services of a lawyer. But long before then, Enitan and Ade Bantan's relationship had already reached a stalement.

Enitan went to town telling everyone who cared to listen that she had been ripped off by a pastor. On one of those rounds, the taxi cab she was riding in ran into a terrible traffic jam. All of a sudden, she felt she needed to use a toilet urgently. There were no public toilets on the bridge where the cab was stuck. She kept yelling at the taxi driver that he should do something because she needed to relieve herself badly. The driver said there was nothing he could do and they had to wait until the traffic flow became better. It didn't get better and droplets of perspiration sprouted all over Enitan's body. She hissed and cursed and tetered on the brink of losing control of her bowels. The traffic crawled sporadically after prolonged intervals of being at a dead standstill, and it didn't get any better. Enitan looked at the silky blue dress that reached just below her knees. She couldn't hold back anymore and completely lost control. Minutes later, the stench hit the driver's nostrils and be began to insult her.

Bitch! If you've soiled my seat with shit, you'll have to have to wash this car or pay for me to take it to the car wash. Can you imagine the bitch, shitting in the car in broad daylight. What cheek!

Will you shut your big fat mouth? I've been telling you all the while that I needed to use a toilet, but you did nothing.

What could I do? Should I have held out my palms so you can shit on them?

Just take me home and let me change.

The car crawled along as flies attracted by the stench assaulted Enitan and the frustrated driver. The driver

231

continued to fret and fume. When they got to Enitan's residence it was already sunset. Enitan refused to come out of the car in her soiled state. She shouted for Sumbo to come down to her. Sumbo couldn't hear her calling, so Enitan sent a couple of kids who were playing in front of the building to go and fetch her. Minutes later, Sumbo came down and Enitan told her to go and get a bed sheet to wrap herself in. Sumbo did as she was told and quickly returned with the sheet. When Enitan got out, they driver came to the back to see if the seat had been soiled. It was too dark to make out anything, but Sumbo gave the driver far more then the actual fare so he could take the car for a professional wash. She then followed Enitan upstairs to the bathroom. No one in the compound knew what had happened, but even if they did, Enitan couldn't care less.

The simmering confrontation between Enitan and Papa Osaze finally broke out early one evening when she demanded that he refund her money and take back his broken piece of junk. As usual, he refused. In anger, she told him she would make him rot in jail and she didn't mind if she had to sleep with every cop and attorney needed to achieve her aim. She had said this with Ade Bantan behind her back. She had momentarily forgotten he was there. Then she turned around and their eyes met. It was apparent she regretted what she had said but the damage had already been done.

In a flash, Ade Bantan now understood why Enitan confused memories of her other lovers with theirs. He now undertood why she ascribed strange rooms and incidents to him. It occurred to him that every one of her memories of romance was interchangeable to her and it did matter as long as she had a man. A man was a man was a man was a man as long as he met her needs. Ade Bantan was merely a statistic in a long series.

This knowledge was hard to digest. Ade Bantan wanted to leave as soon as possible. He decided he would leave like a phantom without explaining his reason. There was no point in continuing to endure the existential cul-de-sac in which he found himself. If he tried to explain anything, Enitan would convince him she had uttered those revelatory words in a fit of anger. She would argue they didn't mean anything, and as such, should be promptly disregarded. But Ade Bantan knew she couldn't explain why she could not remember a single incident of shared memory from their long past together. She couldn't explain why she passed through the lives and memories of men without taking care to file her mental mementoes accordingly. Was she in a tremendous rush to reach a goal? This, Ade Bantan couldn't tell. He just knew he had to leave as soon as possible.

One evening, he left the apartment taking one final look at the couch. Enitan, Sumbo, Joshua, and Susan never saw him again. No one knew where he went.

Ade Bantan fled, albeit it momentarily, from the bleeding couch he had made his home. But there was a void lodged deep within his heart that only Enitan could remove, a void whose warmth he now fought against because he didn't have enough love, tolerance, and stamina with which to feed it. He ran from that dark monumental orifice so he could receive great gulps of air in his heated, congested lungs and he felt ashamed that he had fled the battleground without so much as a word of farewell. He just allowed himself to be sucked into the immense, opaque night, vast and nameless.

Enitan would keep the key to the void in his heart over seas that beckoned her to drop it without a second thought.

He, on the other hand, kept the treasure trove of their joint memories, which his disappearance would destroy with the blink of an eye.

He had to flee from a sinking neighborhood riddled with vigilante gates, orphaned street urchins, and cacophonies that didn't make sense and perhaps weren't ever meant to. Enitan was ready to fight her way out as a good mother hen, but Ade Bantan just couldn't hang around for much longer. He didn't think he had a place amid her huge assortment of relatives, friends and hangers-on. Everyone seemed to have an idea of who he could be and not who he actually was. But he knew he would be a disappointment to everyone and the earlier they knew the better.

Printed in the United States
By Bookmasters